THE
FIXER

N GRAY

VINCI
BOOKS

By N Gray

The Dana Mulder Suspense Thriller Series

Deadly Pattern

Devil Mountain

Chasing Evil

Nightcrawler

Horror

What's for Dinner

Creature Features

Monster Features

Thrillers

Lady Killer

More from N Gray

writing as Natalie Michaels

Steve Campbell Psychological Suspense Thrillers

The Last Girl

The Bone Forest

The White Dahlia

I See You

Death in the City

More from N Gray

writing as SD Syns

The Diaries

Red Lace Diaries

www.ngraybooks.com

Vinci Books

vinci-books.com

Published by Vinci Books Ltd in 2026

1

Copyright © N Gray 2022

The publisher and the author have made every effort to obtain permissions for any third party material used in this book and to comply with copyright law. Any queries in this respect should be brought to the attention of the publisher and any omissions will be corrected in future editions.
A CIP catalogue record for this book is available from the British Library.
Paperback ISBN: 9781036702236
The EU GPSR authorised representative is Logos Europe, 9 rue Nicolas Poussion, 17000 La Rochelle, France contact@logoseurope.eu

Chapter One

MADDOX

It took little to hear my name being called. Those in peril need only whisper '*Fixer*' and I'd hear them. Then I'd snap my fingers and follow the directions to their location.

"Fixer," she called again, more despondent. She's a young woman, alone, and desperately needed my help.

I exhaled and stood up.

"Wait, Fixer, you can't go yet," Jack groaned, blood and spittle looped across his teeth and down his broken jaw. "You didn't do what you said you would," Jack continued in that painful, monotonous tone.

"Jack, I've been lenient with you. It's time to collect." I rolled my shirt sleeves to my elbows. "If you can't hold your end of the bargain, then you know what's going to happen."

Jack whimpered, pushed himself onto his elbows and dragged his body toward the exit, leaving a bloody trail behind him.

"I didn't say you could go," I said sinisterly and closed the gap.

I reached for Jack's shoulder and belt, and in one swift

motion, I threw him across the floor. He skidded, slamming into the far wall with a loud groan and a fresh head wound.

"Please, Fixer, my family—"

"You should've thought of them before asking for my help," I said, stalking Jack.

He cried. The wounds from his forehead, cheek and arms seeping blood, pooling beneath him.

I rarely revealed my true features for fear of hurting, or worse, killing humans. Humans were such fragile creatures, so easily disturbed and pathetic. Few survived the mental break, while others resorted to killing themselves. Only to join my family and fellow demons in the Underworld.

"No, no, no…," Jack continued, his lips swollen. "Please—"

I couldn't wait for him to finish his pathetic sentence. I had enough. The world slowed down. My hands morphed into large, dark claws with sharp, metallic fingernails. My body grew double in size as I watched Jack's eyes slowly widen.

My face darkened into my demonic features—a face only a mother would love—and my horns extended out of my forehead. My black wings expanded behind me and I rolled my shoulders, stretching my neck.

The world picked up speed until the air swirled around us normally.

"No, Fixer, please."

The stench of urine wafted in the air, along with rotten eggs. I narrowed my eyes at his pants, which had darkened near the crotch area.

"Please…" he continued his plea.

"I gave you three chances, Jack. Three!" I shouted. "If anyone found out, they'd stop being afraid. I can't have that."

I lunged at him, gripped him by the shoulders, and yanked him off the floor. I dug my fingernails into his soft flesh until I struck the wall behind him. His screams were music to my ears. His blood fueled my hunger, and I lapped it up hungrily.

I sliced through his meat with my talons, cut through his chest bones, the sound echoing in the cavernous room, and reached for his beating heart.

Jack's eyes rolled back when I squeezed the organ in my hand. The natural pump struggled to beat in my grasp.

Jack's jaw slackened and his last breath escaped his chapped lips.

His dark soul screamed out of his body and I sucked that in. My eyes glowed brightly, like they did every time I fed on souls. The darker the better. My skin tingled and a low growl of satisfaction escaped my lips.

I dropped Jack's limp body, watching it crumple to the floor.

"Maddox!" someone yelled outside, followed by a door blown off its hinges.

That was my cue to escape and follow the moans of the distressed female.

Chapter Two

MADDOX

The distress call sounded from an apartment building in New York. The victim was a mother, holding her child.

"Fixer," she cried, with mascara running down her cheeks as she rocked the corpse in her arms. "Please help me."

I shook my head. The boy was dead; there was nothing I could do to bring him back. I could offer him comfort as he moved to the afterlife in the Underworld; ensure his safety, but that was it.

But to tell a grieving mother was like sticking a hot coal in her face. They wouldn't hear a word I said, only the breaking of their heart.

"He's gone, my dear," I whispered.

Her cries softened as she clutched onto his body, mumbling words I never wanted to mutter. Words begging for forgiveness. Words filled with heartache. Words filled with remorse.

I didn't have to punish her. She'd do so on her own and repeatedly until she joined her son.

I couldn't watch the depressing show any longer and glanced around her two-bedroom apartment, which was small yet cosy. The kitchen neat with a half-filled mug of coffee on the counter.

The living area was large enough for a couch, coffee table, and television. On the coffee table beside the mirror, laced with a white powder, sat a loaded gun, and empty bottles of beer.

A large, naked man from the waist up sat on the couch near the narcotics and weapon, scowling at me.

I arched an eyebrow, and he quickly averted his eyes.

When he glanced at the drugs, he wiped his dirty nose with an even dirtier finger and proceeded to snort a line, not caring I was there. But before he could bring the rolled up note to his nose, I smacked the mirror out of his hands and watched it shatter on the floor.

The man darted out of his seat. I pushed my metallic index nail into his neck, drawing blood. The man froze. His eyes wide as saucers, his blood dripping down his sweaty, hairy chest.

"Don't test me. I'm hungry," I said, sniffing near the man's bald head. "Although I'm not that hungry, your stench and rotting soul would only give me a stomach ache."

The man shook with fear the moment I yanked my fingernail out of his flesh, but he dared not move. His eyes remained on mine, his mouth parted in a surprised O and his blood oozed out of the fresh wound.

I stepped backward and blinked. His shoulders relaxed slightly, and he exhaled.

"Is that yours?" I pointed at the white powder.

The man nodded slowly without taking his eyes off me.

"I didn't know the boy was home—"

I raised my hand, silencing him. "I don't want to hear it. It's yours. The boy is dead. Therefore, it's your fault. Do you agree?"

His eyes flitted to the woman and child on the floor, then back to me.

"Is it your fault?" I yelled, making him flinch.

"Yes… yes, it's my fault," he cried, finally realizing his blood was running down his body, and pressed a dirty hand to the cut. "But—"

"No!" I closed the distance, grabbed him by the throat and squeezed.

The man gripped my arm, trying to pry me off him.

My vise grip needed more than just human strength to get me off him and squeezed tighter; like squishing a grape. I crushed his larynx and broke his spine.

The man seized to exist, his black soul seeped out of his pores like dark ink and I didn't consume it; my cousins in the Underworld could have their fill of him. I dared not taste this disgusting man.

The woman behind me sobbed louder upon seeing her husband's demise, let go of her dead son and crawled to his corpse.

"What did you do? Now they're both gone. How can I carry on?"

"You should've thought of that before calling me, dear," I growled, crouching near her quivering body. "Now about payment," I whispered as I looked her over. She was fit, a slender body, a little too much makeup, but I could smear it off her face with my thumb. "What can you offer me?" I grabbed her wrist and pulled her to her feet.

She whimpered from the sudden movement, but the moment I cupped her cheeks, she stilled. It was only us surrounded by my darkness. Her eyes glazed over as I stared at her, forcing her into submission.

I combed my fingers through her hair and her trembling body stilled. She relaxed in my embrace and I brought her closer to my body.

The same stench I smelled on the man I smelled on her, too. I wrinkled my nose and stepped back, letting her go.

She blinked, confusion stamped all over her face, but the moment she noted the man on the floor and her dead son, she wailed again.

I exhaled and shook my head. At this rate, I'd be staying hungry.

Chapter Three

KINSLEY

"Mom!" I yelled, closing the front door. "Rosie? Ben?" I called, crossing the entrance hall and into the kitchen. "Where is everyone?" I mumbled to myself as I opened the fridge door and stared at the contents, but instead of taking out the delicious pudding or the freshly made chicken casserole, nausea made its way into my mouth and I swallowed hard, shuddering at the aftertaste. "Ugh," I grumbled and closed the door.

When continued silence echoed around me, I entered the living area, and ice filled my veins. The grisly scene in front of me cleared my brain of thought and my body of moving.

My dad on the new Persian carpet with a pool of dark liquid beneath him. I couldn't be certain what the liquid was until flashes of the gaping wounds to his head, cheek, and chest filled my mind.

I clutched at my chest, ensuring my heart was still beating, and exhaled a shaky breath.

My mother sat beside my dad with her favorite chopping knife in her bloodied hands. Her bloody clothing shredded with scratch marks on her inner thighs and across her chest like a wild animal had attacked her.

"Mom?" I mouthed soundlessly. I cleared my throat, but it was too dry.

I crossed the threshold but stopped on the edge of the maroon liquid marking the white carpet. Dread washed over me at the repercussions of what lay ahead; flash photography; reporters; police; questions; abuse; rape; murder. At the center were my parents, and everyone would ask where I was when this took place. Why didn't I stop it? Why didn't I help?

I choked on a sob. "Mom," I whispered after finding my voice. "What happened?" I whimpered.

Mom continued rocking, staring at the knife, then at my father's gutted corpse.

"Mom," I said softly and reached for her shoulder. The moment I touched her, she glanced at me with recognition in her emerald colored eyes and her bottom lip trembled.

"He did it again, Kinsley," she said, placing the knife on the carpet, leaving her bloody fingerprints. She glanced at my father, then stood up. "He came at me again," she whimpered, her body shaking as the adrenaline wore off. "He came for me. I couldn't take it. Not again. I had to stop him this time. You know he wouldn't stop until one of us was dead—"

"I know," I shushed her. "I know," I repeated, reaching for her hand. "Let's get you cleaned up. Now where's Rose and Ben?"

"Uh," she said, glancing around. "Your dad gave them the day off. You know he does that when he wants to be alone with me."

The moment I touched her, she burst into uncontrollable tears. I pulled her into an embrace, never wanting to let go. I wanted to hold her until she felt no pain, until she felt safe, and could be herself again.

I couldn't allow my mother to be tormented by the police because she put down the actual monster. I couldn't allow her to be hurt by the rest of my family, embarrassed by the public, and humiliated by the police.

They would tear her down until there was nothing left of her. She would wither away, leaving me. I'd be all alone.

I held onto my mother, squeezing my eyes shut. When I opened them, I glanced around and became nauseated once more. I couldn't…

I needed someone to take care of this. Someone discreet, and could easily dispose of a body or make it look like an accident.

This needed to be fixed. I needed *The Fixer*.

"Fixer!" I said loud enough before I thought too long and hard about it. We couldn't wait for my dad's body to decompose while we thought of a way to dispose of him. The council would ask where he was. He was influential and always in the public eye and people would know he went missing if he didn't respond to messages on time.

I knew going into any deal with The Fixer could get me killed, or worse, destroy my family. But we needed him now. We needed him to take care of this. Whatever the consequences were, I'd deal with them. Just as long as I kept my mother safe.

I swallowed hard. Wind whipped my face, although the doors and windows were shut.

Mother cowered beside me. I wrapped my arm around her, pulling her closer, and covered my stomach.

A thick darkness spread from the light fixture and

descended, materializing into a man with an ominous shadow. He lifted his head higher and glared down at me like I was dessert. His eyes flitted to mother, then to father's body. A sinister smile crept up his face. It was then I realized I made a mistake.

Chapter Four

MADDOX

I couldn't help the grin splitting my face in two. This was priceless. An affluent family in Sterling Meadow with ties to the supernatural council would afford me more favors than I ever wanted, ever needed. This was the deal of the year.

"You rang?" I sang, staring down at the distraught mother and daughter; the Cavenaugh's.

The daughter, Kinsley Cavenaugh, held her head high, followed by a curt nod. "Yes, I called. Can you make it look like an accident?" she asked. "And ensure nothing points to me or my mother?" She pointed a manicured index finger at the body on the ruined carpet.

"Honey, I can do anything. But what's in it for me?" I asked, folding my arms.

"What do you want?"

I didn't know; not yet, anyway. I didn't need riches, but I loved secrets and favors. "When I know what I want, I'll collect."

The lines between her eyes deepened, and she shook her

head. "Unacceptable, by then you could ask for something I couldn't give."

"Don't worry, I'll ensure it's something you have. I'm fair," I said, crouching near the body.

"Fine," she grumbled.

"Where do you want this sent?" I pointed at the corpse and stood up.

"I don't care. Make it look like a car accident or whatever; just as long as his body doesn't stay here, nobody else gets accused of a crime they didn't commit, and the police don't come after us. Do you understand?"

"I understand perfectly, my dear," I said, stepping closer.

She flinched when I reached for a lock of her honey colored hair; the strands like silk between my fingers. There were fine blond streaks among the sea of warm brown hair, which accentuated her heavenly features.

My nostrils flared at her heavenly scent. I sniffed. Moved closer to her and exhaled with relief; her natural fragrance addictive and enticing.

When a sour smell wafted in the air, I knew it was the mother; fear did that—it messed with a human's body, making them repulsive to my sensitive olfactory sense.

But the girl... She... she was all strawberries and cream. It made my stomach rumble with joy.

"I'll do this," — I swirled my finger in the body's direction, — "make it look like an accident and the police will rule it as so. That way, you and your family will inherit his fortune and nobody else gets harmed. When it's all done, I will be back for what's owed. Understood?"

"Yes, it's fine, just do it," she snapped.

I'd only heard of Kinsley Cavenaugh and her influential

fae family, but I'd met none of them. If I were to believe the supernatural grapevine, her dad was a tyrant, her mother submissive, yet it was she who had taken a knife to his body and removed his heart—a fae's true death.

I wanted to know more about them and what had happened. But if I were honest with myself, I wanted to understand the woman who smelled of strawberries and cream; a sweetness so enticing it amazed me nobody had claimed her as theirs yet.

I reached for the mother but Kinsley slapped my arm away. Not only was she beautiful and smelled divine, she was feisty as well. I liked them with a backbone. I'd only get irritated if a woman couldn't decide for herself.

"I know what you're trying to do," Kinsley said, narrowing her pretty green eyes at me. "And no, you can't see what my mother did. What I can tell you, my father had abused her for years, and today she finally stood up for herself. That's all you need to know."

I pursed my lips; not liking the fact that this tiny woman pushed me away with ease. But I would reluctantly agree and not touch the older woman.

"Fine, but if there's anything suspicious, I will see for myself. Now go, I have work to do."

I watched Kinsley and her mother walk slowly out of the room and disappeared down the hallway.

When I was sure they had gone, I turned towards the corpse. Using enough of my dark power not to alert others I was using, since it was potent enough to broadcast my whereabouts.

I waved my hand in a circular motion, jumpstarting my dark power. In seconds, I'd removed all traces of blood. The knife rose into the air, clean, and placed in its spot in the kitchen. The body glowed as it changed to look like a car accident victim and not one carved from hate.

Then I snapped my fingers; me, the body, and his luxury vehicle left the property and reappeared on Devil's Bend; a corner notorious for car accidents and leaving the occupants dead.

Chapter Five

KINSLEY

After the Fixer disappeared with my father's body and one of our vehicles, I carefully walked Mom up the stairs. My heart ached watching her struggle to do even the simplest of tasks. She'd kick the first step, unable to hold on to the balustrade, or bumped into me. I held her tightly around her waist as we slowly traversed up the stairs.

Once we reached her ensuite bathroom, she glanced at herself in the full-length mirror and paled. Her bottom lip trembled as she fumbled with her torn blouse.

"Let me help you," I said, gently removing her hands from the garment and unbuttoned for her.

She exhaled audibly and dropped her arms to her sides. Her shoulders sagged as her blouse crumpled to the floor.

With her clothing drenched in my father's blood, I picked up the blouse and placed it, along with the rest of her clothing, on the bathroom counter to discard.

Once she was naked, I opened the shower taps until the water was pleasant and helped her inside. She stood under the water and just zoned out. Her chin had stopped trembling, her tears were no more, but I couldn't help but feel what she was going through.

The trauma she'd experienced at my father's hand was insurmountable. She was braver than I could ever be. For years she had accepted her place beside the tyrant of a man who held prominent positions within the supernatural council; positions we all knew he abused but said and did nothing about. We were all too afraid.

I glanced over my shoulder at my mother's portrait, hidden carefully behind was my father's safe; surrounded by impenetrable steel. There were things in there my father kept on everyone. Information I had to keep safe, and possibly use if I had to. To protect my mom, I'd do anything and everything.

Mom moaned.

I turned toward her in time to catch her from falling. I helped her sit, grabbed the sponge, adding liquid soap and washed her back.

She clutched her knees, squeezing her face between her legs, and started rocking.

"It's okay, Mom, I'll take care of everything," I said, washing her back and shoulders. "Can you continue washing or do you want to sit?"

Without answering, she took the sponge out of my hands and washed her shins, then her knees. She straightened her legs and washed her thighs. When she got to her arms, she scrubbed the blood stains off her skin until her arms were pink.

She needed to do this on her own in order to move forward. She had to take that first step in the right direction or she'd give up. I couldn't allow her to lose hope, not when she'd gone through so much and survived to tell the tale. I wouldn't allow it.

When she finished washing herself, I helped her stand, poured some shampoo in her palm to wash her hair.

With her body thoroughly rinsed, I helped her out of the shower, wrapped a towel around her body, and dried her hair.

As we walked past the basin, she glanced at her ruined clothing; quickly I blocked her view and just about pushed her out of the bathroom. She said nothing. I was sure she understood what I was trying to do.

I grabbed underwear and loose fitting clothing for her and helped her dress. Then, while I blow-dried her hair, she yawned and sagged into her chair.

When she was ready, I helped her to bed, offered her a drink of water and gave her prescription medicine that helped her sleep.

Golden rays of sun splashed across her bedding. I picked up the remote, pressed the button that closed the thicker curtains, blocking out any light.

I kissed her forehead, tucked her in, and switched off the bedside lamp.

I cleaned any red marks that were left behind in the bathroom, picked up her clothing, switched off the light, and closed her bedroom door.

In the basement, I threw her clothing into the furnace and watched the clothing ignite and burn until there was nothing left.

A calmness I'd never experienced had seen me through the day and helped me take care of Mom. I was grateful I could, and I'd do it all over again.

I was glad he was gone; my mother's clothing no more. And whatever lay ahead, we'd get through together.

Chapter Six

MADDOX

Devil's Bend was notorious for taking souls. It was one of those sharp curved roads where drivers had to adhere to the speed limit or they'd end up at the bottom of the cliff, broken, bruised, and in ninety-nine percent of the cases—dead.

I glanced around the area; fresh tire marks visible on the road with the new barrier already missing one part with the addition of a vehicle bumper crushed against a tree.

A dark soul floated beside that tree, staring at me. It seemed curious; it knew what I was, but couldn't fathom how sinister I truly was.

A necromancer wouldn't be able to discern whether it was a male or female since it appeared as an apparition; a dark cloudy substance floating, with only its dark orbs for eyes seeing but not truly knowing. I knew what had happened to this lonely soul, but right now, he wasn't a priority.

Without pulling too much power, I snapped my fingers and the luxury Mercedes appeared; crushed and ruined by the fake accident, leaving a trail of vehicle parts on the road before dumping it onto the rocks below.

The black soul flinched, dissolved, then reappeared on the other side of the road; in order to accomplish that, he had to have been here for some time. Few souls lasted before realizing they needed to go to the Underworld if they wanted peace.

I didn't worry too much about the lost soul seeing me or what I was doing. He wouldn't know how to speak, let alone describe what he saw. Nobody would hear him anyway.

I snapped my fingers again and the old corpse appeared beside the crumpled vehicle on the rocks below. His death would appear as an accident, nothing more, nothing less.

I pulled out a burner cellphone and dialed 911, telling them about an accident I just witnessed, where it happened and then hung up. I crushed the cellphone in my hand until there was nothing left but dust, wiping my hand on my black pants and rounded my shoulders. Time to wait.

The cop car was first on the scene fifteen minutes later, followed by the ambulance. They climbed out of their vehicles upon realizing the car had gone over the cliff. Once they saw the unmoving body at the bottom of the cliff, it was no longer a matter of urgency to save someone's life, but to find and recover the body.

I watched the events unfold like a bad eighties movie. There was always that one cop who took charge, yet nobody followed. I chuckled every time his subordinate ignored him and did as he pleased. The cop did something awful to elicit such a negative reaction. If I could get close enough…

I appeared a foot away from the cop when he rounded a rocky bend where nobody saw us.

He blinked up at me, opened his mouth and screamed, but nothing came out of his mouth when I touched his shoulder. His jaw slackened. His eyes stared into nothing, allowing me to *see*.

Flashes of a kid on the grass, blood coming out of his ears and nose, his eyes vacant. A drunken man sitting on the curb with the cop standing nearby, shaking his head. The drunk was his friend.

Next, I saw flashes of evidence getting lost. The friend getting off on a technicality. The parents of the deceased boy crying in the waiting room. The same cop explaining what had happened. Everybody knew what he'd done, but there was no proof.

I shook my head; there was evil, then there was EVIL; and this cop was as bad as they came. I would enjoy his dark soul when he was ready to join us in the Underworld. I'd take great pleasure in making him suffer first before devouring him slowly.

When I let go of his shoulder, the cop stepped backwards, mis-stepping and crashing to the rocky ground.

He shook his head, his eyes glassy, then immediately crawled onto all fours and threw up near a thorn bush.

"I'll see you soon," I said in a sinister tone, disappearing before he turned his head to see who had spoken.

I reappeared near the same tree I had hidden behind before and watched. At least this cop was lazy and wouldn't investigate too much; but my work was clean—always. There was nothing for him to find. This was, after all, only an *accident*.

The cop, Detective Denis Allen, stood up, wiped his mouth, then felt the fresh cut above his left eyebrow from the thorn bush. He glanced nervously around, but nobody paid him any attention.

Denis straightened his shirt and tie, coughed into his

hand, and approached the same junior officer who had ignored his requests earlier.

"James, take over?" Denis barked, with a hint of anxiety in his tone.

The officer seemed taken aback by the request, nodding. "Yeah, sure," he said. "Why though?"

"I'm giving you a chance," Denis said, smiling, but it didn't reach his eyes. "You're always saying you want the chance. Now I'm giving it to you. Don't you want to—"

"I do, but you just insisted you'll be writing it up," Officer James Mercer said, thumbing at the broken barricade behind him.

"Well, I… I… changed my mind. I think you're ready." Denis slapped the younger cop's back and headed towards his vehicle before James could respond.

James whistled and shook his head, grumbling something under his breath I couldn't hear. He continued with his duties, making notes, talking to the coroner who confirmed the victim died because of a head injury but would know more once he'd conducted the autopsy.

I didn't think I had to stay. I'd follow up on James and Denis tomorrow or the next day to ensure the case closed quickly.

As I readied to leave, I heard the faint calls of someone in distress.

Chapter Seven

MADDOX

The call's location was not where I had originally thought it would be. The faint cries of a woman calling my name should've been somewhere near Chicago, yet I ended up in Detroit, Michigan.

I stepped onto the curb leading to a rundown factory; broken shards of glass littered the ground. A burned-out car sat against the broken-down wall where three vagrants sat around an open flame, warming their hands.

The men ignored me as I passed and entered the factory. Inside was the skeleton of a production factory where they had most likely built cars in 1960.

The metal-framed carcass stood like a prehistoric dinosaur and inside its carved out stomach were remnants of worker desks and turned over chairs. A thick layer of dust covered the quickly vacated room.

The floor area still held various ancient machinery with large metal arms and parallel metal rods where they had pushed vehicles from one station to the next to assemble the cars.

"Hello?" I called, my voice echoing.

Silence.

A nervousness I rarely felt crawled up my spine near my neck, leaving the hairs standing on end.

Whoever had called wasn't here and probably never in trouble. Someone else had called, and they didn't want me to know who until I arrived.

I did not like this.

I exhaled, reached behind my back and pulled the dagger from its hiding place, squeezed the handle and kept my back near the exit.

I heard his wide stride and heavy footsteps before he spoke.

"Maddox," Levi said in his sinister monotone.

I rolled my eyes, turning in time to watch Levi stroll through the doorway like he owned the dilapidated place. My eyes flitted to the side, then back at Levi, who wore a smirk I wanted to scratch off.

Levi's modus operandi was to walk in slow motion wherever he went; similarly to those action movies where the main character's coat billowed behind him and his hair was perfect.

Levi wore his signature charcoal suit with a waistcoat, silver pocket watch and trench coat that billowed behind him like an invisible person was holding it out for him, ensuring it didn't touch the ground.

I rolled my eyes. "Do you smuggle invisible minions to do that for you?" I pointed at his trench coat.

The lines between his brows deepened. He glanced at his coat that continued to billow behind him even though he'd stopped walking. When his eyes met mine again, his smirked widened. "I don't kiss and tell."

"Thank Father. I'd rather die than have you kiss me. Now what are you doing here?" I groaned.

"The family wants you home," he said, stopping in front of me.

"In case they didn't get the memo when I ran away from home. I'm not interested," I said, stepping backwards and turning slightly to the side.

"You've had your fun, Maddox. It's time to come home."

"I'll never go back, Levi, not without a fight." I'd rather go down in a blaze of fire, swinging a machete and a flame thrower before returning home. I squeezed the handle and my hands morphed into black claws.

Levi's wings expanded behind him, shadows played on his face, morphing his sinister features.

His expression fueled my anger, and my wings opened behind me, anticipating his attack.

Levi lunged, aiming for my throat. I swatted him away with my dark talon and scratched his forearm. He retaliated with an elbow to my jaw before moving to the side.

I rubbed my aching jawbone. Stars filled my vision as rage overwhelmed me. I wanted to make Levi hurt. As he moved to the side, I flew into him. It was only once we slammed through the half-brick wall, did I feel the pain in my side.

Levi grinned, his pointy teeth bloodied from puncturing his lip. His dark eyes bled to black, leaving nothing of the white. His horns appeared out of the side of his forehead and charcoal-colored baby feathers floated slowly around us.

The pain seared through my body like the fire of the Underworld had latched onto me, dragging me down into the darkness.

I had to get away from Levi before he brought me down permanently. I vowed never to return to the Underworld and would rather die than have him succeed.

I reached for him before he grabbed the dagger stuck in my side and wrapped my talons around his neck. The moment my cold talons touched him, he flinched, then stiffened.

"No," he gasped as I sucked the air out of his lungs and squeezed his neck harder. His skin beneath my fingers hardened as dark scales formed. "Stop!" Levi struggled out of my grasp, but I was always stronger than him ever since we were kids.

I gritted my teeth as I pushed my thumb into his larynx; he gasped for air as the hardened scales spread down his neck and chest area.

The dagger in my side burned through my flesh, tearing into me like Father had promised if I left his side a second time. It was then I knew I had to leave him and the family business. I hated following orders and especially from him or one of my brothers.

"No—" Levi moaned before dissolving into thin air, no doubt wanting to get home where Father could heal the wounds I'd inflicted.

The moment my brother disappeared, I yanked the dagger out of my side. I thought my insides oozed out of the wound, but I wasn't bleeding. There was nothing.

I blinked at the silver dagger in my hand; the handle moved like liquid mercury while they made the blade of a strong glass. Engraved in the handle were markings Seth, my Father, created to punish humans by inflicting a stain on their soul preventing them from leaving the Underworld.

I shuddered at the thought of being stuck there,

tortured by Father, Levi, and the rest of my brothers and sisters. I could never go back.

My palm heated. The glass knife vibrated. I closed my hand around the handle. It stilled before it shattered into a million pieces. The silver handle melted into my hand, then oozed out of my pores and onto the ground.

I shook my hand and wiped my palm on my clothing. I'd never seen Seth's knives do that before.

I needed to reflect on what my next move should be. Levi was closing in on me and knew how to summon me undetected. For now, I would ignore distress calls. I'd starve, but there were other ways of sating my hunger.

Chapter Eight

KINSLEY

It's been a day since my mother had killed my father and she was still in bed. She refused to leave the comfort of her duvet unless she needed the bathroom. I didn't blame her. She killed the man she had loved at first until he abused her. She needed time to process what had happened and if she needed professional help, then I'd get it for her.

"Mom," I whispered, brushing hair out of her face. "I'm going to fill the repeat prescription the doc sent over," I said, waving the script in my hand.

Mom opened her eyes and nodded slowly.

I took that as a sign she understood. I didn't want to bother her any longer than I needed to and left her alone.

Our family doctor had referred her to a psychiatrist. I'd make her an appointment if she didn't get out of bed by the end of the week. I told Mom about him, but I didn't think she registered what I said.

I drove towards the pharmacy and found a parking spot right outside. Once inside, I handed Mr. Medley the script. He had owned the pharmacy ever since I could remember.

"Kinsley!" someone said behind me.

Instinctively I cowered, but then I stood straight, raising my chin as I glanced down at him — Barry.

"What do you want?" I asked with a bite in my tone.

"Aren't you happy to see me?" Barry said, closing the gap.

I raised my right hand, "Stop right there," — I pointed at the blocks on the floor, — "You can't come closer."

"Oh? Can't I?" He taunted and took another step towards me.

My mind went blank. The restraining order was still in place—

"My lawyer appealed the order and let's just say the judge agreed with me," Barry said with a smirk.

I balled my hands into fists, itching to hit him, but he wanted that. He wanted me to hurt him so he could use it against me.

I shook my head, not believing his words and unable to speak.

"And do you know why I did this?" Barry stepped close enough for me to smell the beer on his breath and his body odor; expensive clothing could never make him smell or look better. His mean streak always shone through like a beacon.

I flinched when he raised his hand to tuck a strand of hair behind my ear.

"I know you're pregnant with my child, Kinsley. The nurses at the hospital were helpful by letting the congratulations slip out. You know you should tell them when bad things happen to you, otherwise they'll never know to stay away from me."

My breath hitched in my throat. He knew.

"Is everything all right, Kinsley?" Mr. Medley asked,

separating Barry from me with his arm, then stepping between us, forcing Barry to step back. "Perhaps it's time you leave, Barry. You aren't welcome here," Mr. Medley said with his back to me. I didn't know what their confrontation looked like, but I was glad Mr. Medley had intervened.

"I'm going," Barry said, raising his hands. He turned around and headed towards the exit. "And Kinsley," Barry said over his shoulder. "I'm going to be part of my baby's life, whether you want me to or not, or I will fight you every step of the way." Barry slammed the pharmacy door as he exited.

"Are you okay?" Mr. Medley asked as he turned around.

"Yeah, I'm fine," I grumbled. "Thanks for this." I raised the bag with Mom's medication.

"Sure, next time email me the prescription and I'll have it delivered to your mom."

"Thanks, I'll remember that."

I left the pharmacy and headed straight for my car. As I climbed inside and glanced into the rear-view mirror, I saw Barry sitting in his car, watching me.

Chapter Nine

MADDOX

I parked my Mustang in my reserved parking spot and approached Gipsy's side entrance. Loud music slammed into me when I entered. Niki had the DJ turn up the volume on purpose; loud music usually kept the patrons from leaving—the longer they stayed the more they drank; All Niki cared about was the bottom line, which I could never fault him for. I taught him everything he knew.

I greeted Marc, the bartender, who had his hands full making cocktails and offering the females his charming smile. It didn't hurt he had a magnificently sculptured body, but as always, no human was perfect and Marc was a few lightbulbs short.

I didn't know what to do first, shower, drink, or fuck; or better yet, all three at the same time. My smile stretched across my face when I saw my regular.

"Candy," I said, knowing that my voice elicited a certain reaction from her.

Candy ignored the burly man trying his luck. But Candy wasn't like that, even though her name suggested one thing;

easy. She was genuine, and needy for a certain type of man —like me.

"Maddox," Candy said, her eyes flitted to me, then she turned her body towards me.

"Hey," Burly Man said, reaching for Candy, but I grabbed his hand before he could touch her and squeezed. The bones in his hand crunched in my grasp, and Burly Man cowered.

"Don't you know it's impolite to touch a woman who doesn't want your filthy hands on her." I pushed his hand towards him and let go. Burly Man fell backwards, nursing his broken hand. "Now get out before I make you cry while you confess your dirty thoughts to the crowd."

Burly Man struggled to his feet and darted towards the exit.

I turned to face Candy, who continued staring at me with hungry blue eyes.

"Hmm, you are delicious, my Candy-cane," I purred near the shell of her ear and watched goosebumps spread across her skin. She was a tasty treat and just what I needed to sate my appetite.

Candy followed me to my apartment downstairs in Niki's basement. Niki had taken over the nightclub from someone else and with my guidance transformed it into one of the most successful nightclubs in Sterling Meadow. My payment, he built a secret apartment downstairs for me.

When I reached Niki's office, I waved my hand over Candy's eyes and they closed, followed by her becoming my walking, sleeping girl.

I grabbed Candy by the hand once more and guided her through the hallway towards my secret doorway, then down the tunnel towards my open-plan apartment.

As we entered the vast room, the smell of leather and

aftershave wafted in the air. Candy stiffened when she smelled it too, making me smile.

I waved my hand over her face once more and her eyes flitted open.

"I haven't been here in a while," she whispered, then exhaled. "Would you like to begin?" She didn't wait for my answer as she crossed the floor towards my play area, leaving behind a trail of clothing save for her high heels.

"Present yourself," I demanded. But instead of going to her, I poured myself a stiff drink, downed it and poured another one. I splashed warm water on my face, removed my shirt and noted the area where Levi had stabbed me; there was no mark, yet I still had pain in my side.

I exhaled a frustrated breath and downed my whiskey. I pulled on a fresh T-shirt and headed towards Candy, who kneeled on the soft mat.

I glanced at Candy's toned body and grunted in pleasure. I loved her body; it was so in tune with my play and she always presented herself beautifully for me; like a painting or sculpture for me to look at and praise. A body to worship and please.

Candy's braided hair hung neatly behind her back. Her spine straight as she kneeled with her arms behind her back in a box shape. Her chest was open for me to see her breasts clearly with her knees closed, leaving to the imagination what her little budding flower looked like. Although I'd seen her before, it still excited me to see her this way. A new present for me to unwrap and enjoy.

I grabbed my riding crop and tapped lightly against the inside of her left knee. Candy parted her legs slightly, giving me access to what I wanted. I smacked her lightly between her legs; she whimpered in pleasure.

"Stand," I commanded and approached the X-cross.

Candy stood with poise, her head slightly down and her eyes focusing on the ground as she neared. She turned around and raised her arms.

I fastened each wrist to a corner, then each ankle. Her breathing hitched with every click of the restraints. Her body trembled, anticipating my every move. Her pleasurable fear sent blood directly to my groin, leaving me hard and wanting more.

With the riding crop in my hand, I smacked each breast softly at first, then harder. With each strike, she flinched and her breasts reddened. I continued hitting one breast, then the other until both were rosy, warm to the touch, and Candy moist between her legs.

I placed the crop back in its place on the wall and grabbed the nipple clamps; placing them gently on each nipple. Candy moaned with desire, but didn't complain.

Once the clamps were tightly on, I grabbed the magic wand and forced Candy to cum hard and often. I didn't stop when she asked or pleaded. I stopped when I was ready.

Twenty minutes had passed, and I had an exhausted Candy on her knees, bum in the air, and her face on the mattress. I'd played enough with her and now I needed release.

I slowly eased inside her slick slit and reveled in the sensation of her clenching around me as I pushed all the way inside. I gripped her hips to keep her where I wanted her and continued my delightful assault on her body.

I continued my rhythm as I listened to Candy's moans, like music to my ears. The remnants of the day left my body and my concentration on the woman before me. When the smell of our lovemaking filled my nostrils, I drove deep inside of her. The sound of me slapping against her brought a smirk to my face.

Candy's orgasm struck hard, and I pulled out, driving my cock into her puckered dark hole. She enjoyed when I fucked her backdoor, and I loved the sensation of her ass clenching around me.

I continued my rhythm and thrusted deeper inside her. When my balls tightened and Candy moaned in ecstasy, I pumped her with my heated seed.

After I pulled out, I fell against the bed, pulling Candy with me. She cuddled beside me, exhausted. I rubbed her tender breasts and left delicate kisses on her face and shoulder. I may be rough with my playmates, but I always tended to their needs afterwards. It was the least I could do for the joy they brought me—and Candy was no different.

Candy was half asleep when Niki stormed into my apartment, swearing in Russian.

"Shh," I said, kissing Candy one last time, wrapping her in a soft blanket. She didn't move from her spot, but a soft mewling sound coming from her told me she was comfortable.

"I need your help, Maddox," Niki said, thumbing behind him. "Guess who's back."

Chapter Ten

MADDOX

I was an asshole leaving Candy to recover on her own, but I'd done it before; she knew what to do if she needed me. But Niki needed me.

"You owe me, Niki," I said, following him through the back entrance of his nightclub.

"Yes, yes, I always owe you. You know I'm good for it," Niki said nonchalantly, waving his free hand in the air, and pushed open the fire escape doors.

Seven men stood in a semi-circle, each holding a weapon. The men wore matching teardrop tattoos on their cheeks and similar black clothing.

The leader of this Russian Mafia stood front and center with his hands on his hips and sporting a shiny toothy grin; no doubt he'd received a dental grill for his birthday.

"Nikolai, so good of you to bring your little friend. He's small to be your bodyguard, no?"

I frowned at the comment; I was the tallest man here.

"Mikhail," Niki said, moving closer to his enemy. "We made a deal—"

"I want more," Mikhail said to Niki, but stared at me. I scowled at the little man. Yes, he was one of the meanest Russian Mafia men around, but he didn't know what I was. I stepped closer. He blinked, then his eyes flitted to Niki.

I grinned, knowing I made him uncomfortable.

"No," Niki said, crossing his arms over his muscular chest. "I pay enough to use this building." He waved his hands in the air.

"But you get more people since opening—"

"Only because I run a respectable nightclub, Mikhail. When you ran it, it was full of bad men selling dangerous drugs," Niki said, stepping closer to Mikhail.

"What, you don't sell drugs?"

"Not your drugs."

"Okay, girls, I've had enough of your bitching," I said, pushing Niki out of the way and pointed a finger into Mikhail's chest. "And you," — I said, pushing my finger harder into his pec muscle, — "are testing my patience." The moment my finger touched his cheek, I saw the reason he was here and laughed. My laugh came out blood-curling.

Mikhail's men aimed their weapons at me for touching their boss, but I didn't care. But I worried about Niki. They could shoot me and I'd still live. They'd kill Niki. I still needed him.

Once Niki was behind me, I puffed out my chest and stood a head taller than Mikhail. I'd seen the reason for Mikhail's visit and knew he couldn't afford to hurt Niki even though he would if threatened.

"Tell me what you need, Mikhail. Whatever it is, I assure you I will deliver for a small fee."

Mikhail's shocked expression softened somewhat, then morphed into an angry scowl. "You touched me," he said, sounding dreamlike and confused. He raised his hand towards the spot I'd touched on his face and I was sure it was warm.

"I know why you're really here, Mikhail," I said with a wicked wink.

Mikhail swallowed so hard I heard it and watched his Adam's apple bob up and down. I smiled. The lines between his eyes deepened.

"Oh, come on, don't be shy now that I can give you what you want." I leaned close to his ear and spoke so only he heard, "Whisper it to me. Your men will never hear it, nor will I tell anyone. I will help you in exchange for a favor when I need one."

Mikhail turned his head slightly, and I felt his breath against my neck. "I need to repay a debt by the end of tonight or the Russian mafia will kill my family there," Mikhail said in a hushed tone.

I understood why Mikhail would never admit defeat. Here in the US, he was a formidable force and nobody pushed him around. For him to admit his debt and could do nothing to stop it until he paid was no small feat.

And he accepted my help.

I snapped my fingers and a large bag of money appeared beside Mikhail's left foot. He flinched at the bag, then visibly relaxed.

I grabbed his shoulder and squeezed and with my face near his I said sinisterly, "Don't fuck with Niki again or I will make sure you and your Russian buddies perish most painfully." For his eyes only—my demonic features flashed and Mikhail backed away, tripped over the duffle bag and crashed to the concrete floor with a solid oof sound.

Mikhail's men stormed me, but he waved them away, yelling in Russian to keep away from me.

After a moment, Mikhail stood, brushed the sand off his

pants and picked up the duffle bag. He nodded curtly at me, shook Niki's hand, and told his men to fetch the cars.

Mikhail backed away slowly, his eyes still on me, squeezing the bag's handle.

I raised my hand and pretended to shoot him with my fingers, then blew out the smoke from my index finger tip.

"Don't forget what I said," I said with a wink and spun around. "Come, Niki, I need that drink you promised me."

Chapter Eleven

KINSLEY

I pulled off the bloody gloves and dropped them in the medical waste bin, washed my hands twice and wiped them dry with a paper towel. I grabbed another paper towel and wiped my face.

"I don't know why you put yourself through that. It's not like you need to work," Stacey said, washing her hands beside me.

"I enjoy helping others. And I know I don't have to work," I grumbled. "It doesn't mean I'm not affected by what goes on here."

"Quit. You can if you want to—"

"Mind your own business," I said harshly. I exhaled a shaky breath and shook my head. "I'm sorry, I didn't mean it."

"No, you're right," Stacey said, facing me. "But I've seen how it gets you down. Every time one of them goes, a little piece of you crumbles and dies. You're losing your spark. Shouldn't you prepare for him?" She pointed at my stomach.

I smiled sadly. "Or her."

Stacey grinned. "Or her."

"You're right," I said, nodding. "I must prepare for the little one. And take care of my mother now that my father has gone."

"Exactly, and right now, your plate is full. All this can wait," she added, waving her hand in the air.

Stacey and I weren't the best of friends, but we were friendly, and today was no different when it came to her and one of her speeches.

"I don't want to stop working. Perhaps I can ask to cut down on the weekly shifts."

"Management won't mind, and besides, they love having you around. You can dictate to them what you want and they'll still pay you the same salary," she smiled.

"Thanks, you always know what to say." I squeezed her shoulder as I passed. "I'm heading out for lunch. You want anything?"

"Nah, I'm good, thanks. I'll see you at your next shift."

I grabbed my handbag out of my locker and left the nurses' change rooms.

I didn't get far; Mandy, the Head nurse, cornered me near the exit advising me that Detective Allen had called and wanted me to head down to the station regarding my father's accident.

Detective Allen had visited us the day of my father's *accident*, letting us know they had found a body matching his description and would investigate the circumstances around his death.

My stomach knotted, and a cold sweat washed over me. I imagined the worst; that the detective had discovered what my mother had done, and they wanted to arrest her for murder and me as an accessory.

I wiped my damp palms on my pants and thanked Mandy for the message.

I had two choices, I could either go to the detective and feign innocence, or I could run. Running would make me look guilty, or worse, they would know we were guilty. But the guilty always ran.

No, I had to go. I had to pretend everything was okay. We couldn't afford the police becoming suspicious; not now, not ever.

The Fixer had promised me he would ensure we remained safe from suspicion; I had to believe he was right. I had no other option but to trust in him.

I headed towards my vehicle and called Mom's house phone with my cell. I spoke with Rosie. She said Mother was still in bed and would most likely stay there for the rest of the day. She also said that nobody else had called the house. It relieved me to know the police hadn't brought her in and I could go to them without worrying about her.

I had to believe The Fixer did what he promised, and there was no evidence involving my mother.

I took my time driving to the police station. I parked and strolled to the entrance. When I arrived at the front desk, I asked for Detective Allen.

I barely waited two minutes when a man appeared, looming down at me.

"Miss Kinsley," he said, proffering a hand. "Lovely seeing you again. I'm sorry it's under these circumstances," he said, trying to smile, but it seemed forced. The detective was in his late forties, more salt than pepper hair, and hard brown eyes; reminding me of someone who had a hard life, or had seen things nobody should see. His body reed thin, with sweat stains marking his clothing.

I stood and shook his sweaty hand. When he let go, I

wiped my hand dry on my clothing, thankful I wasn't the only one with damp hands.

"This is only a formality," Detective Allen said, pushing through double doors then holding one side open for me. We traversed down a hallway and entered an office. "You remember Officer Mercer." Detective Allen pointed at a much younger man with brown hair cut short and kind brown eyes. Officer Mercer stood up from behind his desk and shook my hand. "Please have a seat," Detective Allen said, directing me to an available chair near the two desks.

The detective sat across from the officer. Neither one seemed impressed with the other and I wondered what had caused it. I always thought detectives sat together, yet he sat with a junior officer.

"This is just a formality. Normally we'd visit the family to let them know the outcome of the autopsy but because nobody has identified his body, we need you to do that today."

I swallowed hard, nodding.

When Detective Allen and Officer Mercer came to the house two days ago, my mother and I were too distraught to accompany them to the medical office to make sure it was my father's body. And I tried not to think about it since then. I didn't know how I would handle seeing my father's body after I'd already seen it stabbed and his heart removed. I wondered how The Fixer put his heart back without resurrecting him.

"...Miss Cavenaugh," Detective Allen said, his hand near my face.

I blinked at his fingers and glanced up at his face. I didn't see him or Officer Mercer stand.

"If you'll come with us. We'll try to get this over and done with as quickly as possible."

"Yes, of course," I said, standing. "Can you tell me what happened? You mentioned it was a car accident?" I asked, needing to get information out of him without sounding too obvious.

"From the skid marks on the road and the vehicle's recorded drive, we suspect your father had either fallen asleep at the wheel or was driving too fast and braked too late to make the turn," Officer Mercer spoke for the first time. "Unfortunately, we see this happen all too often. We've advised the relevant agencies to look at that stretch of road. Perhaps your father's death won't be in vain and they will finally do something about that road."

We fell silent as I followed them down a flight of stairs and into the bowels of the medical examiner's office. I shivered at the sudden temperature drop and huddled into myself. I pulled on my jacket and wished I wore something warmer.

Detective Allen opened the second door on the right and kept it open for me. I entered the small room, noting the glass wall opposite the door. Someone on that side pulled the curtain open, revealing a covered body on a gurney.

A bald man wearing a white coat and a solemn expression pursed his lips, glanced at someone behind me and pulled the white sheet covering the body down.

On instinct, I stepped backwards and into someone. I glanced over my shoulder at Officer Mercer, apologized for standing on his shoe, and stepped forward again.

My father's body unmoving, almost fake looking. His skin was pale and translucent, with blue veins shining through. It relieved me not to see the smashed in part of his head and his chest had a definite dent, but the sheet covered it.

Movement caught my eye, and the doctor returned to cover his body once more.

"We know it's your father, but we'd like——"

"It's him," I said, nodding. "That's Dad." I wiped my eyes dry with a tissue and blew my nose. I exhaled a shaky breath and turned away from the glass. "I'd like to leave now," I said, walking towards the door. I didn't wait for either man as I headed down the hallway without slowing down.

Officer Mercer caught up with me and accompanied me out of the building, not bothering with small talk. He seemed content to walk beside me and his company made me comfortable.

As I was about to exit, I turned towards him. We stared at each other; frozen in time where we understood loss without needing to say it.

He nodded curtly, his eyes revealing emotions I didn't think he shared often. "If you need help with anything, please don't hesitate to ask," Officer Mercer said, handing me a business card. "I mean it, any time."

"Thanks," I said, taking his card and pocketing it. "I wonder if you can help me with my ex. I had a restraining order against him, but he has somehow had it overturned. Do you think you can assist?"

"Send me the details and I'll look. My email address is on the card."

"Thank you." I nodded, feeling slightly better. "When I get back to work, I'll send through the information."

"Whenever you're ready," he smiled.

I left quickly and headed for my car. When I glanced over my shoulder, he had already left. I opened my car door and turned around in time. I projectile vomited, narrowly missing my shoes.

I wiped my mouth and stood straight, glanced around, but nobody saw me puke my guts out. If anyone asked, I could blame the pregnancy; it was partly the reason.

I called the hospital as I headed home. I spoke with Mandy, letting her know I wasn't coming back to work that afternoon. I also asked for the rest of the week off. She didn't mind accommodating me, which relieved me.

I needed time to process the events of the week and to help Mom. She wasn't coping at all and if I wanted a healthy pregnancy; I needed to ensure I could cope with everything. I'd be raising this child on my own and I needed police help to keep Barry away. Barry had to stop interfering with my life. If I couldn't get rid of him now, then he'd always be in the shadows, lurking, keeping tabs, and trying to interject himself into my life, my kid's life, and the family business.

Chapter Twelve

MADDOX

It's been a while since I last saw Levi, but I knew he's close. My skin crawled at his presence when we were children, and it always would as adults.

It amazed me he hadn't approached again or tried to trick me into going back to the Underworld with him. It made me wonder what he was up to.

I passed between strangers walking in the opposite direction, their shoulders bumping into mine, but I didn't retaliate. They were human; docile and slow. They were heading to work and miserable. The last thing they needed was a supernatural pissing in their coffee early in the morning.

The hairs on the back of my neck stood up, and I spun around, my dark coat billowing behind me. I narrowed my eyes at the dark figure lurking in the shadow.

Levi.

A human bumped into my back, apologized and continued walking. I crinkled my nose at his stench. A younger woman approached, and the wind blew her hair forward and the smell of strawberries and sour grapes assaulted my nose, forcing me to sidestep out of her path.

I slunk towards the buildings, hiding in the darkness. Once I was away from the humans, the smell of rotting meat, dirty feet, and puke minimized.

I glanced over my shoulder and the dark figure was no longer nearby.

I headed towards my destination, a vintage shop that sold voodoo trinkets and secrets.

"Hello, Mama," I yelled as I entered the shop. The bells on the door chimed, alerting her to my entry.

"Maddox," Mama said as she pushed her hands through the beaded curtains. "I'm not expecting you here today," she said, gliding towards the counter. The moment she picked up a black candle, a flame licked the wick, blazing it.

"You know me, Mama, trying to keep you on your toes."

"What do you need, Maddox? You don't just visit me." The lines between her eyes deepened.

The pain in my side throbbed.

Mama's eyebrows shot up. She placed the dark candle on the counter and approached with care.

"You should've come to me sooner, Maddox," she said, raising her hands near the affected area. She closed her eyes and mumbled her voodoo crap, placing her warm hands on my mid-section. "Ooh," she chimed, then pursed her lips. The stare she gave me forced me to step backwards.

"What?" I asked, touching my waist.

"Nobody can remove that pain, my boy. Your family wants you home badly, and I suspect only they can remove it." She pressed an index finger to her lips and stared at my stomach. "But..." she turned around and headed towards her small library in the corner, where she kept her personal tomes.

"If you know of anything, please tell me," I called after her. "Anything at all."

"Maybe," she mumbled as she paged through dusty books.

I couldn't stare at her while she read, so I kept myself busy looking at the trinkets in her shop; voodoo dolls with all the items, various spells I doubted worked unless Mama performed them, candles, charms, non-magical books, and more.

When Mama was quiet for far too long, I headed towards her books and found the space empty. I wanted to tear down the place until pots and pans crashed in the kitchen.

I stuck my head through the beaded curtain and found Mama preparing a green broth. I shuddered at the thought of tasting the foul smelling goo.

"I hope that's not for me to drink?" I asked, entering her lavish kitchen with new appliances, a stark contrast to her antique shop next door.

"Don't be silly, this is for the animals," she said, winking wickedly.

"You give your animals green gunk?" I asked, frowning.

She harrumphed, ignoring my jab.

After a moment of watching her dish the green stuff into bowls, I finally asked, "Well? Did you find anything in your books?"

"Not really, dear. Your family will have to remove the spell they placed on the blade. Unless—"

"What?"

She stopped dishing and gave me the stink eye. "Impatient little devil, aren't you?"

I grunted, desperately needing to reveal my true self, but I reigned in my anger and closed my eyes.

"Much better. You know what I mean to you, so don't," she said sternly and continued dishing the green stuff into plastic cups. I didn't know what animal needed a cup and thought it best not to ask, either.

I'd known Mama since I ran away from my family all those years ago and she had offered me her home as a sanctuary. She knew what I was, yet she still helped me. The least I could do was not show her my true face; I didn't want her to suffer.

"Although I couldn't find anything in my books to help you," she said, bringing me out of my reverie. "You may seek comfort from a Fae doctor. They might not take all the pain away, but they can remove your discomfort."

I frowned at her suggestion. Why didn't I think of it myself?

"Do you know who?"

Mama laughed loudly.

I fisted my hands, controlling my temper.

"If I knew that, my boy, I would've sent you there. But no, you must find out yourself. I'll make some calls and see if there are Fae willing to help the devil's spawn."

I opened my mouth to complain, but she raised her finger to shush me. I pursed my lips.

"That temper will get you into trouble."

I exhaled audibly.

"Now go, you're messing with my mojo this morning." Mama dropped the ladle into the pot when the green goo turned purple.

That was my cue to leave before she added pain to my already suffering body. But as I reached the front door, I called over my shoulder. "Mama, one last thing. Why do the humans stink lately? Is there something in the air or have their diets change?"

Mama entered her shop wearing a puzzled expression. "What do you mean?"

"The humans stink more than usual. The older they are, the worse they smell."

"Old people need to eat prunes."

"It's not that kind of smell."

"Huh," she said, and went back into her kitchen.

"Well?" I called.

"There's nothing out of the ordinary, my boy. It's just you, and possibly that blade they stabbed you with."

"But humans started smelling before Levi injured me."

"Then it's just you."

Mama frustrated me sometimes, but she also helped, except now. Now she only infuriated me.

"Thanks, Mama, I'll see you when I see you," I called over my shoulder as I left her shop.

Chapter Thirteen

MADDOX

My side throbbed, then when I thought it subsided, a sharp shooting pain forced me to double over. I stood straight immediately so as not to attract any attention. The waves of nausea washed over me, followed by the assault of smells coming from the humans walking past.

I hurried through the sea of bodies, glancing over my shoulder for the dark shadow I felt lurking behind me.

I had to get rid of it; I turned down an alley and headed toward a dark corner, raised my hand and snapped my fingers; sparks materialized and vanished just as quickly, then the alley swirled as I moved through space and appeared near Niki's club.

Behind me wind kicked up empty wrappers with passers-by on the sidewalk. A man locked his store for the evening while others remained open.

Sweat peppered my forehead, and pain shot down my leg. At least the lurker wasn't near me anymore, and if he came to Niki's club, he would get lost. I'd made sure any supernatural couldn't find my apartment in the basement;

I'd used Mama's various trinkets to ward off anyone finding it, and I used some of my potent powers just to make sure they all stayed away.

I entered the club on the side at my private entrance, bypassing everyone, and headed straight for my basement. I sighed with relief when I closed my door behind me, leaning on the door and pressing my palms against the cold metal.

It was a Friday and the club would soon become busy. Luckily, I could tune out the sounds.

I stood in the bathroom and lifted my shirt. The wound had healed; the area inflamed and sensitive to the touch, but I felt scar tissue just below the surface.

I pressed against the area, and it felt as though shards of glass were slicing through my tender flesh, followed by waves of goosebumps flooding my body and I shuddered.

I pinched a large area together to see whether I could feel for anything else and I noticed bumps beneath my skin, reminding me of internal stitches. The only difference was, they moved.

"Ah," I yelled, pulling my shirt down. I hated Levi for doing this to me. I wished they'd leave me alone to do what I enjoyed.

I poured myself a bourbon, but before I could down the heavenly drink, pounding sounded on my door.

"What?" I yelled, yanking open the door.

Niki stood with his fist in the air, ready to strike my door again. "Your lady friend has been asking for you. I suggest you get your ass up there before she breaks things," Niki said matter-of-factly, and disappeared down the dark corridor.

I wasn't in the mood for anyone. But I could use the distraction. I wasn't sure which lady friend Niki referred to.

Then, as I rounded the corner, I saw the nasty princess before she saw me. I jumped backwards and into a meaty brick wall.

"Where do you think you're going?" said the meaty wall.

I glanced up when his beefy hands gripped my shoulders. The giant was all stone and no brain and controlled by the witch downing drinks at Niki's bar.

"Oh, you know, when the Wicked Witch is near, one must say hello," I chimed, glaring daggers at Niki because this was his fault. As the hulk walked me closer towards the witch, I mouthed *"You owe me"* to Niki, who smiled sheepishly.

I yanked my arms free of the brute and touched his forearm. His eyes clouded over, his jaw slackened and started drooling.

"Please don't hurt him, Maddox. You know excellent help is hard to find," Wicked Witch said.

"Tell him not to touch me again or I'll send him far, far away."

"Fine, but only if you call me by my real name."

I turned to give the Wicked Witch a stare. She shrugged. I exhaled a frustrated breath. This was about to get messy and there were too many vanilla humans in the club.

I let go of the meaty bodyguard.

"Fine, Felicity. But don't do it again. You know I'm always up for a fight."

I stepped farther away from the bodyguard as he slowly came out of his mini-coma. His eyes fluttered open, and he grunted. But before he could charge me, Felicity placed a calming hand on his chest and he immediately relaxed.

"That's enough, Billy—"

"Billy?" I asked, flabbergasted. "This guy's name is Billy. He looks more like a Fabio or Hulk."

"Don't be mean, Maddox," Felicity said. "Now," — she slapped her hands together, — "is there some place quiet we can talk?"

"Sure, let's go there." I led the way to the empty VIP area, shooing Niki away. It still upset me he led me to Felicity without telling me it was her—I could've avoided all this.

When we reached the VIP area, Felicity told Billy to stay put, snaked her arm through mine, and we sat in a dark corner. I was up for dark corners with hot girls and nasty sex, but with Felicity, dark corners meant one thing. Trouble.

"You caused quite a stink, Maddox, and now I'm trying to fix it."

"Please tell me which stink you're referring to? Just yesterday I pissed someone off just for breathing near them."

That made Felicity smile; I thought she was going to crack. She never smiled.

"You helped a fellow Russian the other night and because of this, you've started a chain of events that's pissed off many people. And now they've come to me to sort out."

I frowned. "How's that?"

"They wanted Mikhail to fail. They wanted to remove his family from Russia and then remove Mikhail. But you helped him and now he's still in power in the US and his family is still alive."

I exhaled and shook my head. I glanced at the patrons enjoying their time on the dance floor, others downing drinks and all I thought about was their liver and how, by the time they reach forty, they'd wished they had behaved—

I didn't care either way, the more souls I ate the better for me.

"Who wants Mikhail out of the way?" I asked, still not looking at Felicity.

"Their big boss, Maddox. It's always the big boss who needs things to change. He wants to manage the US himself but because Mikhail has an army of Russian soldiers following him, he's too afraid to challenge him or his power while he's still alive."

"I hate politics," I grumbled, then turned towards her. "What is it the big guy wants? Money? The army? The drugs they smuggle in, or is it the women they abuse?"

"It's not that simple—"

"It's always simple. It's the humans who make everything so fucking hard." I flew up in one swift motion and paced. "What happens if I can't help?"

"They'll burn down this place with Niki and all his men, including Mikhail, but before they do that, they'll torture them slowly that they'll beg to die. You don't want to fuck with these guys, Maddox. Devil or not, there's too many to fight at once and they don't just have me on their payroll. They have some serious supernatural's who could take you on."

I knew she was right. I could fight many, but with this pain and no way of relieving it, I didn't know if I could manage or survive the attack.

"So what do you need from me?"

"They only want Mikhail." Felicity's expression told me a few things; that they wanted Mikhail dead, and they wanted it done yesterday.

"There will be a war."

"Not your problem."

"You'd think that, but it is. If they kill more than originally planned, my father will hear of it and he'll send my ass down there so fast my head will spin."

"You have twenty-four hours to do it, Maddox," Felicity said, standing. "And my boss wants results, or he'll have my head too." She glared at me so that I saw in her eyes she was telling the truth. Although she was a tricky witch, she never lied to me.

I wrapped an arm around her shoulder and kissed the top of her head. "You know I'll never hurt you."

"I apologized Maddox. It was a misunderstanding." Felicity snaked her arm around my waist and hugged me quickly, but her attention was on her security guards staring at us.

I hated politics. It always fucked with me one way or another. I let go of her and called Niki over.

"I'll see what I can do about Mikhail," I said, reaching for the bottle Niki had brought over and enjoyed a long sip of the honey-sting. My throat burned as I swallowed the liquid. When I emptied the bottle, I threw it against the wall; it shattered, and the glass rained down on patrons sitting nearby.

"Maddox!" Niki yelled.

I shrugged.

Niki offered complementary drinks to those hit by the flying glass and medical treatment for those bleeding.

Felicity shook her head disapprovingly. "I'll check in tomorrow, Maddox. Don't disappoint," she said as she descended the stairs, waving her hand over her shoulder, dismissing me.

I didn't want to kill Mikhail, and I didn't want to be stuck in the middle of a Russian and supernatural war or my family would find me. But something had to be done.

Chapter Fourteen

KINSLEY

Mom sat in her chair and stared out at the view; a picturesque landscape fit for royalty—which was us. I kissed the top of her head. She didn't blink.

"Did she eat?" I asked Rosie.

"Yes, I wouldn't be doing my job if she didn't."

"I know you take care of her, Rosie. I just wanted to know if I needed to feed her when you leave."

"I feed her, bathe her, made sure she's in clean underwear and clothing. She only sits like that after dinner," Rosie said, pointing at Mother. "I make tea then I go home."

"Thanks," I smiled sadly and sat across from Mother. "I've moved into my old room," I said when Rosie left. I, too, glanced over at the rolling mountains. What I didn't tell Mother that I'd left Barry. I wanted to tell her the day my father had died, but it was less important at that moment after discovering his bloody body.

We sat in silence for what felt like an hour, but it was roughly ten minutes. I raised my chin, feeling like a sunflower as I followed the heat from the sun.

"What did Barry say?" Mother asked, pulling me out of my daydream.

I glanced her way, my mouth parted in a surprised *O*; she hadn't moved but her mouth remained slightly parted.

"This is what I need to do. You don't need to worry about Barry. He can take care of himself."

"Rosie is taking care of me until your father comes home from his business trip. Barry will want you home with him."

My stomach roiled as waves of nausea crashed into me like a hurricane.

"Mom—"

"Tea is ready," Rosie said, entering and setting the tray down on the table between Mother and me. Placed neatly on the tray; covered triangle sandwiches on a plate, a pot of tea, and two cups and saucers. "I leave now. See you in the morning," she added, squeezing Mother's shoulder.

Mother patted Rosie's hand like she usually did every day, with a thin smile on her face. "See you tomorrow. Thanks for helping around the house," Mother said, not taking her eyes off her view.

Rosie raised both eyebrows. I grinned. Ever since my father's death, Mother had uttered no words apart from the occasional grunt or moan.

Rosie gave me two thumbs up and left the room.

I poured tea into our cups, added milk and placed sandwiches onto a small plate, handing it to Mother while her tea cooled. I dished up for myself and we sat in a comfortable silence.

When our tea cups were empty and the sandwiches eaten, I helped Mother freshen up and into bed.

I traversed down the stairs and just as I reached the ground floor; I jumped back onto the first step. A figure stood on the other side of the frosted glass door. They weren't doing anything apart from standing there, waiting. Why they didn't press the doorbell was beyond me.

"Hello?" I called, cautiously approaching the front door.

"Kinsley, open up."

I cringed.

"Go away, Barry." I pulled Officer Mercer's card out of my pocket and dialed his cell number.

Barry banged on the door; his football ring hitting the glass making that high pitch tapping with the banging.

"Stop it, Barry," I yelled as Officer Mercer answered the phone. "Oh, hi," I said when he spoke. "It's Kinsley. You gave me your business card."

"Hi, what can I do for you?" Officer Mercer said, his tone sounding distant, like he was working on his computer or something.

"Remember I told you about my ex?"

"Yes."

"He's at my home right now, banging on my front door and refuses to leave."

"I'll send the nearest patrol car over and I'm on my way. Give me your address."

I told him my address but remained on the cellphone; I felt safer knowing someone was listening in case something happened, even though he couldn't do anything about it.

"The police are coming, Barry. I suggest you leave." I grumbled, placing my free hand on my hip. "How did you get into the yard?" I asked, the lines between my eyes deepening. I surmised he jumped over the fence or slipped through the open gate when Rosie left.

Barry didn't answer, instead I watched the door as his shadow disappeared. I reached for the door handle. As I touched it, the buzzer sounded for the main entrance.

I glanced at the small screen and a police car idled outside with two police officers. I buzzed them in and watched the main gate swing open.

I reached for the front door again but didn't open it. I waited for the officers to arrive. When I didn't hear their footsteps like I should've, I stared at the small screen and pressed the button to view all the cameras outside. As I browsed through the various camera feeds, I finally saw movement; two officers chasing a dark shadow alongside the house, and then they were out of view.

Banging on the front door made me jump. I pressed the button on the monitor, and a crisp, clear picture of Officer Mercer came into view. I exhaled a sigh of relief and opened the door.

"Are you injured?" Officer Mercer asked out of breath, stepping past me and inside. There was concern etched on his face.

"Officer Mercer, I'm so glad you're here." My parent's house wasn't far away from the police station, but he arrived in record time. "I'm fine, but there are two officers chasing Barry around the corner."

"Please, call me James," he said, closing the door behind him. "I'll stay here with you," he added, locking the door behind him. "Walk with me while I check the house."

James moved through the house with purpose while I trailed behind him.

"Is there anyone else in the house with you?" he said when he reached the stairs.

"Just my mother."

We checked upstairs, but everything was as it should be, and Mother was already asleep.

"How's your mom?" James asked solemnly once we were back in the kitchen.

"We're taking it one day at a time," I said, switching on the kettle and grabbed two mugs out of the cupboard. "How many sugars do you take?"

"None for me, thanks."

I flinched when someone knocked on the glass door behind me. James stood and opened the sliding door.

"Officer Mercer, I didn't know you would be here," the officer said as he entered the kitchen. "Vincent almost caught the assailant until sparks flew out of his hands."

That caught my attention and placed the kettle back in place. I approached the men, who glanced my way.

"What do you mean by sparks coming out of his hands?" My ex was not supernatural. He wanted to be on the council and did everything to get there. He ensured I fell pregnant; guaranteeing his place in my world. I cringed at the thought of how he had used me, yet elated that I'd finally become a mother. Although I wished the circumstances were different but it happened; stealthing happened to me and unfortunately often to others. When I realized what Barry had done, I knew I couldn't trust him any longer.

"Red sparks flew from his palms and although I'm not supernatural, all the hairs on my body stood on end. And since Vincent is a were-jackal, he continued chasing after him. Whatever the assailant was, he was bad. I could tell Vincent wasn't happy going after him."

"Thanks David," James said, patting David's shoulder. "Do you want to wait outside for Vincent? Maybe he needs backup."

David's eyes flitted from James to mine, then nodded.

Once David left, James entered the kitchen. He finished making the coffee I started, gave me my mug, and had a long sip from his mug.

"Tell me about your ex," James said, his expression tight.

I gave James the short version; Barry and I dated for a year. He proposed within eight months; I said yes, then I fell pregnant. But it was only when I caught him with his secretary and found many videos with him and others doing sexual acts I'd never seen before did we split. After I ended the engagement, Barry turned into any woman's nightmare. A stalker.

When I had Barry arrested for breaking into my home, he went from pleasant to nasty quickly and things turned ugly. And now he had a judge in his pocket who could overturn his restraining order.

James listened intently, nodding in understanding. Once I stopped talking, he finished his coffee and stood up.

"Guys like Barry are extremely dangerous. And if you know him as human but David saw sparks, then it's reason to be concerned." James removed his cellphone from his pocket, crossed the living room floor and spoke to someone. When he ended the call, he nodded curtly. "I've arranged for a unit to watch your house. If Barry tries to enter your premises again, we'll arrest him."

James first ensured that David and Vincent returned unharmed, and the unit watching the house arrived before he left.

David and Vincent took my statement, spoke to the other officers, and then they, too, left.

A shudder ran through me after the men left, the house locked tight, and it was only Mother and me.

If Barry had somehow changed into something else, I feared what it could be. I'd heard of others experimenting with DNA of supernatural's and turning humans into powerful creatures and in the name of science or for war.

An army capable of regenerating human flesh, or fought non-stop without needing rest, all highly sought after.

I switched off the lights downstairs and headed upstairs to my old room, where I'd already unpacked my things. I entered my bedroom, stopping dead.

Barry towered over me, his eyes glowed red and a sheen covering his skin. His expression stopped me, forcing me back into the hallway, but I didn't get very far.

Barry lunged for me, knocking me to the ground and all I saw were stars.

Chapter Fifteen

MADDOX

The blood moon, along with the millions of diamonds in the black night, shone brightly down below. While monstrous buildings caused deep shadows large enough for demons to hide in.

I crouched between a dumpster and the wall; the shadow absorbing me and I waited. A security guard headed towards me, his attention on the surrounding dark fence.

As the guard closed the distance, I stood from the darkness like the demon I was and swiped; removing his head from his body, using my long, dangerous talons. Blood sprayed, ruining my new black shirt.

The guard's head flew; I caught the silent, screaming meaty skull before it hit the dumpster. In that split second, I nudged his limp body, ensuring it fell on the soft grass, eliminating the sounds of a body dump. The last thing I needed was a loud noise alerting the rest of my unwanted presence.

This was not how I envisioned my evening would go. I'd

much prefer having Candy bent over my lap, her pretty ass in the air, begging for my hand to slap her supple cheeks rosy. Instead, I was here, doing what I despised with all my might.

Although I had options; I couldn't swoop in like a bloodthirsty vampire or snap my fingers and use the dark power I'd been born with—which was like using magic—it would cause chaos. It would only alert my family I was pulling power, and they'd swoop in and grab me.

The supernatural creatures surrounding the mansion were talented fuckers, and they'd sense my approach before I said abracadabra. They sensed magic before the user bothered opening their mouth.

It forced me to use my brain and obviously my brawn instead. I fisted my talons, my metallic nails receding.

I needed my stealth mode to finish this. I craved precision and calculated risks; as the devil's spawn, I understood danger. All it took was one idiot to make a hurried phone call to someone else and they would summon the cavalry. Literally. These idiots had a direct line to my side of the Underworld.

None of that would do.

Now, with one guard unable to call for help, I had one more to remove from the equation before I grabbed my prize. I spied my target eating and watching football.

The guard I needed to destroy first stood beside my target, ensuring no harm came his way.

Surveying the grounds one last time for danger, I flew to the third-floor balcony when it was safe.

I padded softly towards the open sliding door, my target and his guard engrossed in the football.

I had to kill both at once. If I didn't, I would only kill my target and then I'd have to fight the guard; which would cause a ruckus because this guy was not only hulk-huge, but powerful, too. Our fight would alert the other guards, then I'd have to fight them, and if there were too many, I'd have to fight with my demon power—which I hated using.

It was one thing showing a client my true demonic form to ensure he didn't fuck with me, but it was another using power to defeat other supernatural's. It would alert my family to my location like a beacon; a bright light highlighting my face like a target for a hunter.

No. I had to use other means to kill this guy and hopefully settle old scores.

I exhaled an annoyed breath and frowned. I needed to be quick, precise, and deadly. So I channeled my secret inner demon, the one my family couldn't detect, and flew inside the room.

The huge hulk saw me out of the corner of his eye first. He started turning his broad shoulders towards me. I screamed silently, raising my hand and aimed my talons for his throat.

I pierced his soft meaty skin before his lips parted in a surprised *O*, my fingers gliding through his bony neck like a hot knife through butter.

My target turned his body towards us, his eyes widening.

With my free hand, I plunged my sharp fingernails into my target's cheek and shoved my fingers down his throat, muting his screams.

The burly guard crumpled to the ground, clutching his throat; it was a futile exercise. He would be dead within seconds.

My target, however, was a tough sucker. He gripped my arm with his meaty hands, trying in vain to remove my hand from his mouth.

I yanked my hand free of the guard's neck with a slurp sound and gripped my target's hand, breaking it.

My target cried silently as I pushed two fingers farther down his throat, blocking his windpipe. Now that I'd broken one of his hands, I pried it free of my arm and went for the other one. When I'd broken both hands and he was turning the same shade as the maroon drops on his cheek, I removed my fingers.

My target fell beside his guard, moaning.

"Where's your book?" I asked menacingly.

My target shook his head, catching his breath.

I gripped his ears and pulled, tearing the tops from his head.

"Please," he mumbled through a thick tongue and hoarse throat. "Enough!"

"Have you ever shown your victims mercy?"

He shook his head.

"Exactly."

I left him to stew in his misery while I searched his desk near his bed. The open plan room had little personal effects and all business. I found the leather-bound book in a secret compartment in the antique oak desk, along with additional deeds for businesses he owned around town.

"Thank you," I said, raising the items for him to see. "I don't like being cornered into doing something I despised, so because you forced me into this, I will take great pleasure in destroying you."

My target's eyes widened. Fresh tears streaked his face while clutching both broken hands to his chest.

My face morphed into my demon features. My target paled. His eyes rolled into the back of his head when I dug my fingernails into his chest and removed his heart.

Footsteps running up the stairs was a sign of my departure.

With the ledgers and organ in hand, I flew out of the room and over the property, heading towards my vehicle.

Chapter Sixteen

MADDOX

By the time I reached my basement apartment at Niki's club, the pain in my side had exploded into a variety of stinging sensations.

A cold sweat covered my skin even after I switched on the hot water and stood under the showerhead.

I needed help.

But that wouldn't happen soon; I first needed to find a fae doctor to ease the pain. Unfortunately, I hadn't had the time to find one yet. There was no phone directory listing the supernatural's and all their talents. I needed to go on word of mouth or a friend of a friend.

I grumbled as I dried my aching body, glancing at the items I'd retrieved. At least my evening wasn't a complete bust, and I didn't see Levi lurking anywhere nearby, ready to strike.

But... soon I'd be hearing from Felicity.

A distress call caught my attention, and it was serious; it had the same flavor of one I'd had before. I licked my lips as a cocky smile stretched my face. Luckily, I had this call to help take my mind off the pain.

I slipped on black jeans, a black dress shirt, socks and my black leather shoes. I was still in my gothic phase and doubted I'd ever leave it. As I reached the front door, I donned my charcoal trench coat.

I followed the direction the call had come from, to stare at the beauty I'd helped almost a week ago. Only this time, something terrified her.

The ominous man looming over her opened his hands, revealing glowing palms, reminding me of demonflame. The hunger in his aura left me on edge. I didn't like this situation and had to intervene. Whatever or whoever this man/supernatural wannabe was, was dangerous.

I tasted the air and his flavor was strictly human, but the demonflame in his palms told me otherwise. Either he was summoning a demon or one was using him. Regardless, both scenarios were dangerous.

I noted the man knew Kinsley. And she knew him.

Kinsley's eyes flitted to me when I appeared.

The threatening figure stood straighter, his neck clicking, and slowly turned his head. His human brown eyes glazed over as the demonflame reflected a deep red in his pupils.

"Someone called," I said cheerfully. My side throbbed, but I dared not show this subhuman someone had injured me or he'd use the opportunity.

The man-demon grunted.

"Cat got your tongue? Or is that demon?" I didn't want to give him the upper hand and lunged for him. My long fingers circling around his neck. The moment my icy hands touched his skin, scales formed.

The man's eyes focused on me, shrieked and battled out

of my grasp. I let him go. He fell to the ground and scooted away on his ass.

"What…," he said, swallowing hard. "What happened?" he spluttered, tears forming in his now conscious eyes. He glanced at Kinsley, his head shaking. "Did I hurt you?"

"What was that, Barry? You tried to kill me," Kinsley said, touching her stomach.

I thought I heard something the first time I met her. Narrowing my eyes at her tummy, I heard a slowing heart beat deep within her body.

Blood covered Kinsley's left temple and her swollen shut left eye. Her lip had split and a bruise already formed on her cheekbone. Barry had given all his punches to her left-hand side.

Barry had beaten her within an inch of her life, but she was stronger than he thought. She called me just in time.

I suspected the attack was because of the life she carried —the now bruised and dying life; it was only a speck, but it was a baby—barely holding on to this world; a cruel world full of monsters. There wouldn't be much the baby would miss, apart from motherly love.

As much as I hated admitting it, I doubted it would survive the day.

I considered Kinsley; her heavenly features. She seemed soft and fragile. Her green eyes glowed because of the sclera, now red from Barry choking her—evidence marking her throat. Her light brown hair with blond highlights caked in blood.

Kinsley had gone through so much this week already; her mother killed her father for reasons I could only imagine. Usually when a woman murdered her husband, there was a good reason for removing his heart. There were few

female killers, although they were out there, it was predomi-
nantly males who killed.

And now her ex had tried to kill her.

I hoped she didn't want an easy way out—a direct path
to the Underworld where we kept those souls who had given
up, in a place no soul should be. It was horrid and tortuous.

I didn't have the heart to tell her that the tiny being
inside of her may not make it, that I couldn't help him, I
couldn't bring him back.

Resurrection wasn't something I could do. My dark
power could only rearrange those already dead. My dark
power contained no light. I had no light left to give.

Barry pulled himself to his feet, backing up into a room.
"I only wanted to reach you, to tell you I loved you. That I
didn't want to lose you. But... but," he mumbled, combing
his fingers through his disheveled hair.

"Who possessed you?" I asked, closing the gap. If he
tried to run away, I'd grab him.

Barry stared at me as if seeing me for the first time. He
stared at me so hard I felt it like a weight against my face.
He thought about my question and didn't seem to know the
answer.

"Well?" Kinsley demanded, bringing Barry out of his
daydream.

"I can't recall his name. He bumped into me when I
left you the other day," Barry said, staring at Kinsley.
"Then I woke up with him," — he pointed at me, —
"trying to kill me." He buried his head in his hands and
cried.

I exhaled and pulled the man-child by his left arm,
popping his shoulder joint.

Barry shrieked in pain.

I lightly touched his forehead and visions of the man

he'd bumped into came into my mind's eye. Levi. Dammit. I let go of Barry, who crumpled to the ground.

"Stay away from Kinsley," I said to Barry. My tone harsh. "If you see the same demon, best you run in the opposite direction. He will abuse your soul until there's nothing left, and you haven't even reached the Underworld yet."

I approached Kinsley, glancing at her wounds once more.

"You need your injuries seen to."

She shook her head. "I'll be ok," she said with the faintest of smiles.

Not knowing what she meant, I turned to Barry again. "I suggest you leave and never come back. If you bother her again, I'll make sure your life ends painfully."

Barry nodded and headed for the passage. He glanced at Kinsley, then quickly averted his eyes. He mumbled something to her as he passed, then darted down the passage and stairs. The front door opened and closed.

Kinsley pressed numbers on the keypad in the other room, arming the house. When she entered the bedroom I remained in, her wounds had lessened.

I pointed at her no longer swollen eye. "Self-healing?"

Kinsley touched her face, and her smile broadened. "Yeah, something like that. I'm a nurse at the hospital," she said, then her smile wavered. "It doesn't always work. When it's their time to die, they go." Her words held sadness. She genuinely cared for the ill and took it upon herself to do everything she could to save them.

"Are you a fae healer?" I asked, remembering her father being a fae king and hope fluttered in my chest. The pain in my side flaring.

"I am. Why? Do you know someone who's injured?"

My smile widened. If I was alone, I'd shout 'hurrah'.

"Including today, you owe me two favors. Am I right?"

"Yes," she said, nodding slowly.

"You still owe me for the first one. If you help me, then today's favor gets cancelled." The moment the words left my mouth, I regretted it. I didn't consider the little life inside of her and whether she even had the energy to help me.

When Kinsley caught my expression, her hand went to her stomach and smiled, sighing.

I listened and the tiny heartbeat had returned stronger than before.

"How did you know I was pregnant?"

"I heard the tiny heartbeat. But…"

"I won't lose him," she said amusedly. "It would take more than my ex or a demon to hurt me." She turned and headed for the stairs. "Come, I need to eat before we do anything."

Chapter Seventeen

KINSLEY

I wiped my hands dry on a paper towel and finished my tea. My fae healing abilities easing my pain. The baby I carried was safe once more, and the only thing that let anyone know Barry had attacked me was my dirty hair and dried blood spots on my clothing.

The Fixer explained something had caused him pain in his side, which was hampering his ability to do his job. Although I didn't know what had caused his pain or how it affected him, I had to help. I couldn't leave him to suffer.

The Fixer lifted his dress shirt, and I stood frozen, staring at his muscular body; beneath his clothing, I never imagined a toned body carved with heavenly features. I must've taken too long because he cleared his throat. I raked my eyes up his body, coming eye-to-eye with his warm brown eyes.

I smiled sheepishly and closed the distance. Rubbing my hands together, tiny white sparks illuminated my palms, and I pressed my hands against his hard muscles. His skin was warm against my fingertips.

The healing pulses I pushed into him echoed into my palms and I felt the darkness within. Whatever was causing him pain was like a dark tapeworm burrowing itself within him; inside his veins, muscles, nervous system. Slowly, it was killing him.

I closed my eyes to concentrate as I pushed more pulses inside his muscles, then his veins, and once more into his nerves. The darkness had latched itself onto him like a cancer I didn't think I could cure him of, but I'd at least slow down its consumption.

When I finally removed my hands from The Fixer's body, I pulled my top away from my damp skin. I exhaled a shaky breath as I fought nausea.

"Are you okay?" He asked, his skin paler than before.

"I've been better," I said, sitting on the nearest chair. Luckily, I ate, or I'd have fallen to the ground. "You don't look so good yourself." I smiled. I didn't know The Fixer all that well, but someone had injured him. That whatever had happened to him was affecting him. "Do you still feel pain?"

"It's not as bad as it was before," he said, shaking his head and touching the affected area; which was now a rosy color.

"It reminded me of a cancer," I said, pouring myself a glass of cold water. "It's nothing I'd encountered before. I mean, I've healed many who were stage four, but this," — I waved my hand in his direction, — "is something else. Powerful. Potent. Incurable."

The Fixer pursed his lips, his eyes darkening. He knew who had hurt him, but didn't share the details. It wasn't any of my business. At least I only owed him one favor instead of two.

"When will you collect your other favor?" I asked.

"Soon, but I must go now," he said, vanishing before I responded.

I yawned, exhaustion taking over. It was well past one in the morning and I needed sleep. It was a tough day.

Chapter Eighteen

MADDOX

Kinsley's healing touch was heaven sent. The pain had receded, and manageable. I still felt her lingering touch as if she'd caressed over my entire body; I smelled her natural scent on myself still and I wanted to savor it, bottle it so that I could smell her whenever I needed to feel calm.

There was something about Kinsley I craved. And when she closed her eyes, her hands on my abdomen, all I thought about was kissing her. Her lips pulled in a tight line as she concentrated and even stuck her tongue out; when that happened I wanted to nip at her.

My cock stirred as my thoughts turned from wholesome to dirty, pressing against my pants. The things I wanted to do to her; her wrists tied, her legs spread, and wearing my collar.

A man bumped into me, apologised and continued walking in the opposite direction. I wasn't paying attention to where I was walking; my mind full of visions of Kinsley.

When the hairs on the back of my neck stood on end, I glanced over my shoulder.

Levi.

I froze. I frowned. He glanced left and right—searching as if he knew I was here... somewhere, but couldn't see me.

I didn't understand it. I shouldn't, but I did—I approached my brother, stopping twenty feet away.

Levi looked right through me. Unseeing.

I almost laughed, but didn't want to risk making a sound. I touched my side; my skin still warm where Kinsley had touched. Could it be? No way! I smiled to myself as I waved at Levi, but he turned and walked in the opposite direction.

My smile split my face in two. Kinsley's touch had not only part-cured me, but my brother couldn't see me. This was the best day ev—

Powerful hands gripping my shoulders ruined my thought. I didn't need to turn around to know it was Felicity's guard grabbing me. Oh shit.

"What have you done?" Felicity screamed, following it with a hard slap across my face.

Being the devil gentleman that I was, I didn't hit back. I also knew it was my fault she was in a rage.

"You killed the wrong Russian," she continued.

"Did I? I'm sorry. They all look the same—"

Slap!

"Ow, that one hurt," I moaned, moving my jaw from side to side.

Billy grabbed my wrists, squeezed and pulled my arms back, forcing my shoulders to strain, my neck to twist, and I moaned again.

Felicity squeezed the bridge of her nose with her thumb

and index finger. "Why did you do it, Maddox? You've really caused trouble amongst the entire family now."

"I solved everyone's problems." I smiled, but then blood from my nose dribbled into my mouth and I spat it out, narrowly missing her red high heels.

"Argh," she grumbled, stomping to the other side of the room.

"It's going to be all right. I promise—"

"How can you be so sure? Those now in charge have ordered your death."

"Mikhail will take over the reins and will do no such thing. He owes me two favors already, so don't worry your pretty little head."

"Mikhail? How can you be so sure?" she asked, narrowing her eyes.

"Still so suspicious. Ah," I cried. "Please tell Billy to ease up. He's going to break my arms." I might be immortal but I still got hurt.

Felicity waved Billy away. He released me and headed to the back of the room. She exhaled a shaky breath and chewed on her index fingernail.

I stood up and rounded my shoulders. When I closed the gap, she stopped me at arm's length—luckily her arms were shorter than mine and I still touched her cheek. She leaned into my palm, her skin warm. Any other time I would've pulled her closer and kissed her. Not anymore. Things changed. We changed. She changed the most.

"You know I'll always take care of you." I stepped backwards, giving her space. She always wanted space. "We've gone through so much," I said above a whisper. "You know I'll always have your best interest at heart. I may be a bastard and a killer, but I take care of those I love."

Felicity glanced up, her big brown eyes glistening in the

dim light. For a Wicked Witch, she had a tender side somewhere deep within. The side I fell in love with. And I fell hard. But also like a witch—she was sneaky and had Daddy issues I couldn't tame, even in the bedroom.

"I trust you, Maddox. But please… I beg you. Don't mess with me."

"I know," I said, raising both palms in mock surrender. "You'll see. Someone will let you know it's sorted and you can come out of hiding." I grinned. "I need a drink. Where's your bar?" I asked, glancing around.

"Billy, get him a whiskey, please. And bring me one too."

"Good girl," I said with a salacious smile.

"I'm not your good girl anymore, Maddox," she replied, her lips twitching.

Chapter Nineteen

MADDOX

I arrived at Niki's club only to be accosted by Mikhail in a hug attack, followed by kisses on each cheek. The short Russian was thankful I'd saved his ass a second time.

"Okay, that's enough," I said, pushing him away. "Rather buy me a drink before you touch my ass."

Mikhail burst out laughing and slapped my shoulder. "You're a funny guy."

"Yeah, wait until you hear my Ted Talk."

That set him off more again, and he held his belly, laughing. "Drinks," he yelled at Niki, who hurriedly ensured he liquored us up.

I sat across from Mikhail and Niki, both wearing matching lopsided grins.

"You've saved us, brother," Mikhail said, shoving an index finger into my shoulder.

"You're awfully touchy-feely for a scary mafia guy," I said, finishing my shot of vodka.

Niki snickered. Mikhail backhanded Niki, who almost fell off his chair.

"Sorry, brother," Niki said, nursing his aching jaw.

"The others have joined my ranks, thanks to you," Mikhail added, tipping his head in my direction. "Even those in Russia have agreed. When you killed their fearless leader and they realized who did it, they immediately asked for forgiveness," he said knowingly. "They all fall under me now." He downed his vodka with pride and slammed the glass on the table, spilling Niki's drink. Niki didn't complain this time. "And I owe you, Maddox. Anything. Anytime. You know I will do it."

I nodded, reaching for the bottle of Beluga Vodka and filled our glasses.

"I'll let you know when I need something." I downed my shot, slamming my glass on the table, and swayed slightly, then corrected my posture. Normally, alcohol did little, but this stuff was potent and we were on our second bottle.

Niki downed his shot, got up from his chair, and collapsed, unmoving.

Mikhail laughed, and I joined him. Niki could handle his alcohol; but it seemed the stuff affected him, too. I, at least, was still thinking properly.

Two servers picked up Niki by his arms and dragged him to his office; out of sight, out of mind. With him gone, nobody yelled at the servers.

The kick in my side threw me off the chair and I landed on the ground with a hard thump. I groaned, my abdomen felt like I was being sawed in two.

I glanced around, but nobody had kicked me. Whatever Kinsley did to me earlier was reversed, and the pain was doubly sore.

"Hey, Maddox, you okay brother?" Mikhail asked with concern in his tone. He stood up from his chair, swayed, but stayed on his feet. "Must I call someone?" He slurred, glancing around. His arm absently reaching out for nothing but air, then turned back to me. "Who must I call?" He shrugged.

"I'm fine. Must be your vodka," I said, standing up. My legs wobbled and the pain in my side so severe I wondered if this was what it felt like giving birth. My insides twisted by sharp barbed wire fence.

I needed Kinsley to help me again, only this time she had to stay with me. If the effects wore off each time she helped me, and it returned worse than before, I might not survive. I needed her with me before her magic subsided.

But I had a problem. I hated owing anybody favors. Even though Kinsley owed me one more favor, I wanted to hold on to that one in case I needed her again. She proved to be quite useful.

I needed to come up with a reason she had to stay with me. Perhaps her ex was still hovering nearby, and I had to rescue her once more. I could tell her if she helped me I would continue keeping her safe; that way we kept each other out of harm's way. She would accept that as a plausible reason. Hell, I would.

"Hey, where are you going?" Mikhail mumbled, grabbing hold of the chair, doubling over and puking all over the table. He paled and before he fell, his three guards rescued him.

"I'll check in with you later," I said, squeezing his shoulder. "Get some rest. I can't rescue you just to have you die from alcohol poisoning."

Mikhail snickered as his guards walked him out of the club; at least my new Russian friend and Niki were safe, and Felicity didn't have a death warrant on her head—or on mine.

I glanced around the dance floor and headed for a dark

area where nobody saw what was going on and slipped through space only to appear outside Kinsley's parent's mansion.

I surveyed the area; the police cruiser still parked inside the grounds with the high fence surrounding the property. The immediate area around her house brightly lit, but there were many shadowy areas I could use to move through.

I moved through the darkness. Once I was inside the gated area and out of sight; I approached the side near her bedroom. Her room the only light illuminating. The curtains moved as wind blew in through the open window.

I flew up to the ledge and crouched, silently peering through the window. The shower turned off, followed by humming. Silently, I slipped through the open window and sat on her bed, stretching out my legs, and leaned back on my elbows.

Kinsley opened the bathroom door with a towel wrapped tightly around her body. She froze. Her eyes darting towards the window, then her bedroom door.

"It's okay," I said, sitting up and raising my hands. "Your ex was here again. But I chased him away." I paused, waiting for the information to sink in. "I was thinking of hanging around to ensure he stays away. If he gets that demon to possess him again and comes after you, I don't think you'll survive." I glanced at her stomach.

Kinsley rubbed her abdomen, biting her lip and nodding silently.

I smiled inwardly. My plan was working.

"Would you mind if I changed quickly?" Her eyes flitted towards her bedroom door. "Then I'll prepare one of the spare bedrooms for you."

"I don't need a room or sleep." I lied. The day's events

exhausted me, but I wasn't prepared to let her out of my sight. I flinched when the pain struck again.

"Is the pain back?" she asked, closing the gap. Before I answered, she reached for my shirt, forgetting about her near nakedness, and lifted my clothing.

I glanced down and gasped. Where she'd touched earlier, her hand print remained yet pain laced the surrounding area.

She brushed her fingertips lightly against my skin. I closed my eyes and exhaled. Her touch was a thousand volts of pleasure wrapped in a sensual embrace. My skin pebbled.

"It's worsened," she said, bringing me out of my trance.

"It kicked me off my chair," I added, curling my fingers around her wrist, still pressed against my side. "Your touch helps ease the pain, and you have pushed none of your powers into me yet." I grinned.

"There's a correlation between the power inflicting the pain and you. I don't understand it." The faint lines between her eyes deepened.

I knew exactly what she was getting at, but I couldn't explain my heritage. The less she knew, the better. I shivered when she removed her hand.

"Do you mind stepping outside while I change?" she asked, her tone soft.

I got to my feet easily. The vodka no longer affecting me and the pain had subsided.

"I'll be right outside," I said, pointing at her door.

Once I closed her bedroom door, a loud banging sounded from the other side, followed by running and a few swear words. I smiled slyly, wondering if she was looking for clothing that had the potential to seduce me. I hoped so.

I ambled down the passage, stared intently at each photo featuring Kinsley. Some were born beautiful; a natural beauty so rare and wholesome that drove most insanely jealous. Yet with each encounter with Kinsley, she spoke with kindness mixed with a hint of feistiness. I loved it.

Her bedroom door opened, and she stuck her head out, looking left, then right. When she saw me, she smiled and entered the hallway wearing a cute pajama t-shirt and shorts. There was nothing sexy about it, but it looked cute on her; reminding me of a college student who didn't know what day it was.

"You can sleep here," she said, sauntering down the hallway in the opposite direction.

I watched her ass sashay and had the urge to spank her. My cock hardened; I rubbed myself over my pants as I watched her ass wobble. She was delicious.

Visions of Kinsley tied up in my basement filled my chest with hope. An urge to lick her lips then nibble her chin made me ache to grab her and do naughty things with her body.

Kinsley glanced over her shoulder as if hearing my thoughts, her eyes dark and her cheeks rosy.

Gods, she was going to be the end of me. I shook my head when she glanced away, remembering that I couldn't touch her. Not while she still had a debt to pay me; it was a rule I created, one I never wanted to break—again.

Many years ago, I played with Felicity before she paid me back and I ended up broken-hearted and Felicity had disappeared. I vowed never to make the same mistake twice.

My passionate embrace with Kinsley would have to wait.

"If you need towels or another blanket, everything is

here," Kinsley said, opening a closet behind the door. "Are you hungry?" she asked with a quiver in her voice. She backed up until she hit the door, slamming it shut. "Uh," she mumbled, fumbling with the door handle.

"I ate already," I said, my tone deep and throaty. It was another lie. I didn't need to eat human food. But telling her I sipped on evil souls wouldn't sit well with her.

I stepped closer with purpose, knowing my expression caused her sudden nervous response.

She opened the door while staring at me, then leaned back, closing it again.

I grinned and was sure I had a twinkle of amusement in my eye.

Kinsley turned, pushing her shoulder against my chest, and opened the door once more.

I pressed my arms against the door, caging her in, and slamming the door shut.

She flattened her body against the door, trying to get away without success.

I leaned forward, my face inches away from hers.

"Why the hurry to leave?" I asked, flaring my nostrils. Her scent was enticing. Captivating. Addictive. I wanted to taste every inch of her.

Her chest moved up and down as she sucked in deep breaths of air. Her cheeks rosy and her pupils dilated.

She felt the attraction too; it was unmistakable how her body reacted to my closeness.

I rubbed my nose against her cheek. Her skin soft and warm. Tiny sparks joined us together, and I ached to remove her tight, thin clothing.

She closed her eyes, and mouth parted.

"You feel something for me, don't you?" I asked. My lips

near the shell of her ear and watched all the little hairs on her neck stand on end.

"Uh-huh." She nodded.

"You want to kiss me?" I brushed my lips against her cheek and near her lips.

"Uh-huh," she moaned, her eyes still closed. Her chest continued rising and falling with heated breaths.

I touched her shoulder with my index finger, then traced her collarbone until I reached her neck. Then I moved my finger down between her breasts.

"You like this, don't you, little one?"

"Uh-huh," she moaned louder, nodding her head, her eyes still closed.

"Well, it's a pity you're the only one, now isn't it." I stood back to watch the angry fireworks from my harsh statement.

Kinsley's eyes shot open, frowned as my words sunk in. She raised her hand to slap me, but I caught her wrist before she could.

"I'm the worst supernatural to seduce. I will play with your feelings, abuse your body for my pleasure, and I'll make you beg for more. Is that what you want? One night of carnal pleasure only to be tossed aside like garbage. I will hurt you in more ways than one, little girl. It's best to stay away from me or I will ruin that sweet body." I hissed, letting her wrist go, and stood farther back. "I'm only here to help you because I like favors or secrets. And I want you to keep the pain at bay. That's it. So the only time I'll come to your bed is if I need your hands on my side to ease the discomfort." I pointed at the door. "Now go!" I yelled.

Kinsley burst into tears, flung the door open and exited, slamming the door as her last words.

As she ran to her room, I punched a hole in the door, then fixed it with my magic.

I hated doing that, but I couldn't allow her to get lost with me. I was the worst supernatural for her to mess around with. If my family knew about her, they'd use her against me. I couldn't allow her to fall in the middle of my family squabble. I did it to keep her safe.

Chapter Twenty

KINSLEY

My heart continued racing, my pulse thundering in my ears and my skin damp. I crossed my legs and shuddered from sensations fluttering in my core.

The Fixer had a strange power over me, and I hated him for it. My body responded to him without him touching me. His voice struck my body like a tuning fork and I sang for him.

I hated how my body betrayed me, but I was a foolish girl walking around in my tightest pajamas. Naively thinking he wouldn't say anything. I was teasing him, yet hopeful he wouldn't respond.

I was wrong.

I shook my head in shame. He was right, though. But his words cut deeply and I hated him more. His words were cruel and unnecessary.

I slapped a scatter cushion off my bed and mumbled when my fingers clicked, and sharp pain shot up my wrist.

But… he was right. I had to stay away from him. He needed a warning sign around his neck to ward off women.

But... I thought, biting my lip as the red rope filled my vision, my wrists bound and my ankles strapped to a spreader bar. My core tightened and spasmed, sending another wave of pleasurable sensations.

I abruptly stood up, stomped towards the light switch, and flicked it off. I stomped back to bed, climbed under the covers, and switched off my bedside lamp.

Sleep, that's what I needed. My body required rest following today's events and this evening's excitement. Hopefully, my dreams were boring.

Chapter Twenty-One

MADDOX

I helped myself to some coffee in the lavish kitchen; I may dine on lost souls regularly, but I enjoyed human comfort foods now and then, too.

I watched the tiny house keeper scurry around me, fussing everywhere I placed my mug or stood. I suspected she guarded the Cavenaugh's house with such ferocity she'd put most supernatural guards to shame.

Rosie stood well under my chest, salt and pepper hair tied in a neat bun atop her head, and her black-and-white uniform pristine. She was the model house servant.

With no supernatural abilities of her own, Rosie used what nature had given her—her hands. The three-story mansion ready for visitors, and the kitchen spotless, with ready-to-eat food in the fridge. Yet she continued to hustle and bustle around me like an angry hummingbird.

"Oh, you're up already," Kinsley mumbled as she entered the kitchen. She was still angry following my abrupt statement—good, she should be angry. She helped herself to some coffee and stood far away from me.

"Yes, I heard your dragon lady," — I pointed at Rosie, — "make a ruckus in the kitchen so I had to enquire who it was." I grinned.

"She's not a dragon lady," Kinsley fumed, draping an arm around Rosie's shoulder.

I raised my hands in mock surrender. "We need to go. Grab something to eat and come."

"Why?"

"You're spending the day with me until I get this sorted," I said, pointing to my side.

Kinsley grumbled, stormed towards the fridge and grabbed a small yoghurt and an apple.

"I'll see you and Mom later," Kinsley said to Rosie. "Call me if anything happens."

"Why are you going with this man?" Rosie asked, her suspicious fiery eyes stuck on me.

I grinned, needing to show Rosie my true self, but didn't. I couldn't risk Kinsley seeing that side of me yet.

"It's fine, Rosie," — Kinsley squeezed Rosie's shoulder, — "he's protecting me from Barry."

"I don't trust this one." Rosie wiggled her finger in my direction. I tried to move out of the way, but that bony finger followed me.

"I'd love to stay and prove my worth, but we must go," I added, pointing to my naked wrist for effect. I headed towards the door, grabbing Kinsley's hand as I passed. "Bye Rosie, don't wait up for us."

Kinsley missed a step, but I caught her waist and held her up.

"Easy darling, there are easier ways to fall for me."

"Ugh, get off me," she moaned, pushing me away. "Where are we going, anyway? I thought we were staying here."

"As much as I enjoy staying in your mansion, I have work to do. And you, my dear, need to come with me."

Ever since I'd arrived last night and being close to Kinsley, the pain in my side had all but vanished, and I was thankful I didn't get that kick like I did at Niki's club. So wherever I went today, Kinsley had to tag along, and that meant coming with me when I swapped favors.

I held Kinsley's hand tightly. Her smaller hand in mine felt way too comfortable for my liking, but I dared not let go. I was afraid if I did, she'd bail on me.

"Ow," she cried, prying her hand out of mine.

"Not yet, darling." We stopped near a shadowy corner in her garden where a creepy grew over the high wall and a tree. "Don't freak out, but we'll be moving through space."

"Huh? Wai—"

I didn't give her time to finish her sentence, and we moved through the darkness and out through the other end, near my next client.

"Sherry," I said, approaching the busty blond in a dark tailored dress suit.

Kinsley, paled and clung to my right arm like a little monkey.

Sherry stared down her nose at Kinsley, arched an eyebrow, then looked at me. "What's this?" she asked, pointing a manicured finger at Kinsley.

"That's none of your business. But if you must know, she's my new partner," I quipped.

Sherry harrumphed, spun around and marched towards her place of business.

"What was that about?" Kinsley asked, still clutching my arm.

"If you want to stay alive, say nothing. Do you understand?" Kinsley nodded. "Good, because she won't hesitate to hurt you."

"If she's so scary, why does she need you?"

"Because she doesn't enjoy getting their hands dirty. Now," — I shook her off my arm, then took her one hand in mine, — "don't be so clingy, I'm not going anywhere."

"All right, sheesh, so grumpy."

"Say nothing."

"Okay, I get it," she grumbled.

I smiled, opened the door, and we entered.

Sherry stood just beyond the doorway with her hands on her hips, her red lips pursed and her foot tapping those high heels.

"What's it this time, Sherry? I hope you didn't kill your toy?"

Sherry stiffened, and I knew I'd hit a nerve.

"No way!"

Sherry blinked back tears and pointed towards her room.

"I can't go in there." She shook her head and glanced away.

If Sherry couldn't go inside her room, there's no way I'd allow Kinsley in there. "You stay out here with Sherry," I said to Kinsley. "And don't eat my guest," I said to Sherry. "Or I'll make sure your father hears about everything."

"Come with me," Sherry said to Kinsley, holding out her hand.

Kinsley took Sherry's hand, and the two women headed for the kitchen.

I peered around the doorjamb and stopped myself from throwing up. Red colored the usual dark blue room. It was horrific.

"Sherry!" I yelled. "What did you do to him?" I said over my shoulder. The poor boy's body hung over the table, head and brain matter scattered all over the room. I shuddered, not wanting to know the details. It was painful what he had gone through. The sight was awful. She needed to be taken before a firing squad.

A shudder ran through me as I waved my hand in the air. My dark magic swirled and cleaned the room. The young man's body started sewing itself back together, his body intact, his death an accidental choking.

I cleaned the crime scene with finesse and poise that would make any parent proud. It's a pity Father was such a hard up devil.

When I was content the area was void of blood and other fluids, I headed for the kitchen. I found the two women gossiping in the corner, huddled over mugs with empty plates to the side, and a cupcake in their hand. I narrowed my eyes at Sherry—I could not trust that one.

"I don't want to know what illegal confectionery has been going on," I said with a chuckle.

"Your partner was telling me about the hospital she works at—"

"Don't Sherry, or I swear I will—"

"Easy there, Maddox."

If Sherry approached any patient at the hospital and brought them here to play with and indulge, I had to stop her—permanently.

"Maddox?" Piped Kinsley, hearing my real name for the first time. "Is your name Maddox?"

"What, you didn't know The Fixer's true name?" Sherry asked, bemused.

"No, how would I know."

"True, only those he rescues often enough get to know his name," Sherry said, smiling.

"I wouldn't be too happy, Sherry. Your crime scene was awful. I don't know how you did it, but you need to stop. This is the last time." I warned.

Sherry noted the seriousness of my words and sat back in her chair, averting her eyes. "He said he could handle it. But when…" she swallowed hard. "He tasted the stuff I offered, his eyes bulged, then… kaboom." She made a sound emphasizing the 'kaboom' and used her hands for added effect.

"He was human, Sherry. You of all supernatural's can tell a human from one of us."

"But you know how I get smoking opium."

I shook my head. "No more," I said, raising both eyebrows. "And I'm not kidding. This is the last time I'm saving your ass. Do it again and I'll call your dad."

"Okay, okay, I promise." Sherry raised her hands.

"Good, now lay off the opium and other substances. You know the Sugarplum fairy likes to lace that stuff with her own concoction. If it doesn't kill you, it will make you kill someone. My case in point." I pointed towards her room.

"Okay, enough." Sherry rested her head in her hands and whimpered. "I've asked the Sugarplum fairy not to give me anything, even if I beg and threaten to kill her. I know I can't keep doing this."

"Go to rehab, Sherry. I'm sure they'll make space for you at any of the facilities."

Sherry nodded, knowing I was right. She stood up from the table and exited the kitchen.

"Come," — I proffered my hand, — "I take it you don't

need food." I chuckled at the amount of empty dishes on the table. Kinsley took my hand without hesitation. Her small hand fitting perfectly in mine.

"Where are we going now?"

"One more stop, then we'll go back to your home."

Chapter Twenty-Two

KINSLEY

We swiftly moved through darkness that The Fixer, not commonly known as Maddox, seemed to bend with his power. Teleportation was common amongst my kind, but I'd never mastered it. My dad and mom could do it, but not me, and nobody understood why.

I only had my natural healing ability; which was enough for me. And I preferred using my power for good; saving lives worthy of a second chance. But sometimes they didn't make it. I couldn't cure death, only prolonged the Grim Reaper from claiming his next victim.

I gave Maddox a side glance, his sharp features etched in stone, giving no emotion away. But when he glanced at me, the twinkle in his eye and the curve of his lips told many stories; personal and delightful.

But his conflicting signals gave me whiplash. First, he rejected me, then his kindness, sending my emotions into a whirlwind. Yet I couldn't bring myself to get away from him. I wanted him to hold me, touch me...

My thoughts wandered for a moment. Then reality hit

me in the face like a brick through the windscreen. Maddox had brought us outside a nightclub I knew belonged to Russians. Very dangerous and scary Russian part of the mafia.

"What are we doing here?" I asked carefully.

Maddox didn't answer. Instead, he grinned, squeezed my hand tighter, and opened the door. He moved through the nightclub at record speed, with me running behind him, trying to keep up.

Eventually, we stopped near a wall. I furrowed my brows. I wanted to ask why we stood near a wall when Maddox surprised me by waving his hand, almost touching the wall, when the wall opened like a door.

We entered, and the secret door closed behind us automatically.

"Wow!" I said, entering the lavish, open-planned apartment. It was a typical bachelor pad with dark wood and leather furniture, stainless steel appliances in the kitchen and a large mirror on the ceiling above his maroon colored bed with similar color silk sheets.

I swallowed hard, surveying the large space. When my eyes darted in the opposite corner, I felt my cheeks heat and warmth blossomed between my legs.

"I won't be long, just a change of clothing, then we can go," Maddox said, stripping as he walked to his bathroom that was very open except for the shower curtain and half-wall surrounding the toilet.

Maddox removed his clothing, climbed into the shower and washed his body as if I wasn't there. His toned muscles moved with dexterity, leaving my mouth dry. He wasn't large like a bodybuilder, a more fit swimmer or cyclist. And his ass was just the right shape, very bite-able, or was it nibble-able.

I had to tear my eyes away from the demon in human form and raided his kitchen cupboards. His kitchen was full of food, which was odd for someone who didn't eat human food. I glanced at him from around the open fridge door. The shower curtain moved as he washed his body. My imagination ran wild thinking of the places he touched as he washed himself. I narrowed my eyes, wondering whether he sensed my stare.

My stomach grumbled. I turned my attention to the cooked roast turkey, reminding me of Thanksgiving. I grabbed the plate and closed the fridge door with my elbow and sat at the kitchen counter, ripping sizable chunks of the meat and shoving it in my mouth. It was delicious.

When I'd eaten enough, I covered the turkey once again and grabbed a milkshake out of the fridge door and downed the sweet liquid.

Once sated, I plopped myself on the couch, not realizing Maddox was out of the shower. It was difficult focusing on the coffee table when a very sexy naked man was drying himself, slowly and with purpose. I felt the weight of his dark and dangerous gaze on me. I grabbed the only magazine on the table and leafed through it, ignoring him.

My heart slammed against my chest at the carnal pleasures the other room caused. It was something I'd only read about in romance novels or seen in movies. It got my pulse racing, and I crossed my legs; then I remembered what happened last night when I crossed my legs and uncrossed them. But it was too late. That fluttering sensation, followed by flames of desire, flooded my system and I was sure my entire face glowed red.

I fanned myself as I tried in vain to concentrate on the magazine in my hand. Once I finished paging through the magazine, I stood and walked around, avoiding that room and Maddox. As I was about to open a door near the kitchen, Maddox appeared.

"Ready?" he asked, reaching for my elbow without waiting for my answer.

"We going to my place?"

"Yep," he said, a sly grin splitting his face in two.

Ugh, I hated that my question sounded as if I wanted to do something with him in my house. I thought it best to ignore his salacious expression.

"You don't have to hold me every step of the way," I grumbled, pulling my arm out of his grasp. The farther away I walked from him, the better for me.

"You'll need me when it's time to move through the shadows."

"Then it's fine, but until then, keep your hand off me. I don't need you yanking on my limbs." I folded my arms and walked a little behind him.

Maddox opened his front door, and we exited. The door morphed back into the wall, hiding his apartment once more. I followed him through the maze of a nightclub and almost walked into him when he stopped.

"What's wrong?" I asked, peering around his broad shoulder.

"This way," Maddox said, turning me around. Before I saw what was going on we entered the kitchen.

"Maddox," shouted someone behind us.

Maddox turned around and pushed me behind him.

"Niki, what is he doing here?" Maddox asked the flustered man heading our way.

"You know I can't keep your brother out. He scares me."

"As he should. Your bouncers should've kept him out."

"You know my bouncers," Niki said, rolling his eyes.

"You need different bouncers."

"Yeah, yeah, later. But first you must leave," Niki said, pointing at our exit.

When Maddox turned around, I saw Niki's face. He was pleasant looking, not ugly, but not quite handsome either. He had pockmarks on his face, with a tattoo on his cheek and neck that left me chilled to the bone. Russian mafia.

"And who is this precious little thing?" Niki asked, licking his lips.

Maddox spun around and grabbed Niki by the throat. He pushed Niki up against the wall. Silverware crashed to the floor with a loud clatter.

"Touch her and I'll kill you myself."

"Easy there," Niki said, raising his hands. "I didn't mean it. No worries."

Maddox squeezed Niki's neck harder, his face turning shades of red, then purple. Niki tapped Maddox's hands. After another minute, Maddox let go and Niki crumpled to the ground.

Niki rubbed his throat, sucking in air. "Jeez, man, what's up with that. You know I'll do nothing stupid like that. The woman is yours."

"Nobody can know about her. Do you hear me?" Maddox hissed, his hands bunching into fists.

"Yeah, man, nobody," Niki said, flustered. "Nobody has to know nothing."

"Good." Maddox said nothing else, but his expression said it all. He would kill anyone who knew I was with him. I couldn't understand his reaction if he wanted nothing to do with me. I didn't understand it. Just another thing to confuse me. And I couldn't understand why he was avoiding his brother.

I didn't have time to ask questions. Maddox forced me out the kitchen door and into the parking lot and towards a midnight blue Mustang. He opened the car door for me and closed it once I sat down. He walked around the car when a man approached, glancing left and right—searching. Maddox froze; he knew the man. I assumed it was the man he was avoiding in the club. His brother.

Maddox's brother didn't see him, didn't even look at me. It was as if he couldn't see us. He traversed between the cars and disappeared around the corner.

"Is that your brother?" I asked when Maddox climbed behind the steering wheel.

"Yes," he replied, lost in thought.

"Why don't you want to speak with him? And why couldn't he see us?"

Maddox turned to look at me as if I'd sprouted a second head. "You noticed that?" he asked, frowning.

I nodded.

"Strange," Maddox said, lost in thought again, then finally started the engine. The Mustang roared to life. He shifted it into gear and sped away, fishtailing.

I didn't understand what was happening. Whatever it was, it upset Maddox, but I couldn't help but wonder if it was because of me.

Chapter Twenty-Three

MADDOX

"Why are we in your car instead of zipping through your dark passageways?"

"I might need it later, so I thought I'd kill two birds with one stone." What I didn't tell her was that I didn't know if her moving through my black power would affect her unborn baby. I couldn't have that on my conscious as well.

I parked the Mustang and told Kinsley to stay in the car. I wanted to ensure her ex wasn't here for real before she entered her home.

Rosie greeted me at the door, her eyes suspicious and her mouth in a tight line. It was only when she told me no-one was here except the two cops keeping watch did I allow Kinsley inside.

Kinsley went to her mother's room while I enjoyed a stroll in the garden. The air crisp and although I rarely felt winter, the chill in the air took me by surprise.

The sting on my side left my skin damp. The farther I traversed away from the house, the more intense the pain. I quickened my steps and headed back towards the house. Back to Kinsley.

It frustrated me I couldn't be too far away from Kinsley or the pain returned. I had to find Levi and reverse this curse. But to do that, I had to leave Kinsley home alone. But being away from her left me at death's door.

I couldn't allow Levi or my family to know about her or about her ability. But I couldn't stay in her house forever.

I rubbed my face with my hands, then combed my fingers through my hair. This was a disaster. I didn't know how to fix it. I chuckled at the irony of it all. I could fix everybody else's issues except my own.

Rosie yelled she was leaving, I yelled back, she must leave the cutlery. I saw her giving me the middle finger; I grinned and waved. Then the front door closed, followed by the alarm sounding.

"Must you always tease her?" Kinsley asked, tying her gown tightly around her waist. Tonight she wore a silk robe and my imagination ran wild with what was underneath; nothing, or silk pajamas. Either option would drive me mad.

"She's too uptight. She needs to get laid—"

Kinsley slapped my shoulder, but a smile tugged at the corners of her mouth.

"Or something," I said, chuckling.

"Did you see anyone out there?" she asked, switching the kettle on and removing mugs from the cupboard.

"No, nothing for now," I added, ensuring she remained alarmed. I couldn't allow her to relax and think she didn't need me anymore.

The pain had eased in my side, but it didn't answer my question or how to handle the situation.

I accepted the tea Kinsley offered, chamomile tea fused with honey.

"Your pot-pourri juice is delicious," I teased.

Kinsley laughed. It sounded wonderful. She didn't hold back her delight, instead she enjoyed the moment, and it made me smile.

But when our eyes met, I saw the emptiness within that I'd love to fill. And she saw a side of me I rarely revealed to anyone. A side I'd shown once and was badly burned. It took me years to get over it, and vowed never to fall like that again.

Until now.

I placed my mug on the counter. Kinsley followed my lead. Her lips parted. Her eyes darkened and her heartbeat sped up. My heart raced as I reached for her throat, my fingers curling around her neck. Her eyes closed when I squeezed gently and when I pulled her hair back, her mouth opened. I grabbed the opportunity and kissed her, bruising her lips with mine.

Our tongues tangled in the heated moment. My left hand roamed her soft breasts while my right hand kept her head in place. Kinsley's hands pressed against my chest as if to push me away. But she didn't. She embraced my passionate wrath on her body.

When she moaned, I pulled away and opened her silk gown. I groaned. She had nothing underneath.

"Such a naughty, dirty girl." I winked wickedly.

Kinsley nodded absentmindedly.

"What do you want to do, Kinsley?"

When I said her name, her eyes shot open; her gaze filled with lust as she raked them over my body.

"What do you want me to do?" I asked again, needing her to say the words.

"Kiss me," she said, pointing at her lips. "Pinch me," — she pointed at her nipples, — "and I want you here," — she added, pointing at her naked mound.

"You're mine and I can do with you as I please, but within those parameters?"

"Uh-huh," she said, closing her eyes when I pinched her nipples at the same time.

"Does that feel good?" I asked near the shell of her left ear.

"Uh-huh." Her words barely audible.

I picked her up and carried her to her bedroom, laying her down gently on the bed and got to work pleasuring this incredible woman.

I chuckled to myself as I played her body like a musical instrument, tuning it to bring sounds out of her pretty mouth, and ensured each stroke left her warm and satisfied.

I caressed gently, then applied pressure where necessary. Each mewling sound made me harder. Kinsley's skin soft against my hard fingers, but she enjoyed the rough and pleasurable play.

When I inserted two fingers into her tight pussy, she clenched around me immediately as her first orgasm rocked into her. I continued pumping my fingers into her slick slit and when she came undone a second time; I removed my fingers, leaving her orgasm mid-air.

Kinsley moaned. The lines between her brows deepened. Then, when I pushed the tip of my cock against her delicate folds, she smiled.

"Are you ready for me?"

"Take me," she said, her eyes on me.

I slowly edged the tip inside. Kinsley watched me while I watched her. With each gentle thrust inside of her, she exhaled sharply as she got used to the girth of my steel member.

Kinsley felt incredible as I thrusted into her. She

moaned with each stroke as I kept my rhythm, building that momentum. Sweat peppered her forehead. Her fingers gripped the sheets tighter. And when I pumped harder and faster, she met each of my thrusts with her own. She was greedy and wanted more.

I did as her body craved. With each measured stroke, I thrusted deep within her—harder, faster, until our love-making echoed within the four walls.

Kinsley's orgasm ripped into her, forcing a loud moan, which added fuel to my already burning fire of desire. My orgasm struck. I grabbed hold of Kinsley, gripping her closer to my body.

I slowed my rhythm, my orgasm intense, while Kinsley continued clenching around my cock; it wouldn't be long before I was hard again, ready to take her. But I wouldn't, perhaps another time.

When I felt she'd finished, I kissed the tip of her nose and slowly pulled out. Kinsley moaned from my loss and snuggled into the curve of my front. I didn't have the heart to push her away, and pulled her closer, holding her. I kissed the side of her face, her smile lifting her cheeks, and I kissed those too.

Chapter Twenty-Four

KINSLEY

An urgent need forced me out of the bed and into the bathroom to relieve myself from my aching bladder. My body continued to hum with Maddox's everlasting touch. I tasted him on my lips, smelled him on my skin. I felt where he'd been, and I knew where he was going next. My thoughts caught me off guard as I washed my hands. The intense attraction I felt towards him was suffocating, yet alluring, and I didn't want it to end.

My smile split my face in two as I imagined us walking in the park, holding hands. Or perhaps feeding ice cream to each other. I suspected Maddox was a dark chocolate man while I enjoyed vanilla. Perhaps Maddox would take me out for dinner and a movie.

I rubbed my belly, thinking about the child, and knew it wouldn't work. A man, demon, like Maddox wouldn't settle down with a woman who had baggage. But, as my heart continued to beat rapidly, I silently wished for something a little more. I knew not to expect anything, but...

I opened the bathroom door and froze, blinking rapidly.

Maddox's room. I was no longer in my bedroom, but the room where he kept various benches and devices I'd only seen in documentaries and read in books.

My heart sped up as an icy shiver ran down my spine.

Maddox stood in the center of the room wearing low cut jeans with the button undone. His chest glistened with a fine layer of sweat, his heated stare left me a quivering puddle of excited nerves. He pointed at a black leather chair. I obeyed and sat down.

I waited patiently as he prepared, tying the binds I no longer fought against, and gave in to him with my body, heart, and mind.

Maddox tied the soft, red rope around my wrists above my head, securing it in place. Then he tied each bent leg opened wide, and then tied each leg to an armrest.

My core exposed, my skin naked, my body vulnerable.

I shouldn't trust him; he was dangerous. Spawn of the darkest and evil supernatural being ever. He would only hurt me; torture my soul till the end of days, and, like he had said before—make me beg for more.

The longer I stared into his dark eyes, the more I saw tenderness... and... something else. Was it love? I didn't know. But there was something between us I didn't want to decipher. I didn't want to label it. I just wanted to allow it to breathe, to grow, and watch it bloom. Whatever it was, I wanted it. All of it.

Securely bound to the chair, I waited for Maddox to take what he wanted; what I wanted him to take. What I allowed him to use.

Maddox stood in front of me, his naked broad chest heaving, his cock straining to get out. He was a delicious sight to behold, and I wanted another taste.

I licked my lips.

Maddox shook his head. "So needy," he chuckled, moving closer with a black riding crop in his hand; I ached to feel the sting of it.

I flinched when a jagged knife pierced Maddox's abdomen, blood oozing out of the fresh wound.

A strange creature with scaly skin, horns, and glowing yellow eyes hissed at me. The creature removed the knife from Maddox's abdomen with a slurping sound and morphed into a man as tall as Maddox with black hair cut short, soulless eyes, and wearing black clothing that looked painted on him. It was the same man we saw at the club— the one who didn't notice us in the car. His brother.

I shook my head, mumbling 'no', but the man closed the gap. He was going to hurt me.

I screamed and thrashed around. Strong arms held me down while soft lips kissed my wet cheeks.

"Shh," he said over and over. "It's okay, it's only a dream."

My eyes flitted open to Maddox sitting on me, keeping my arms above my head.

"Are you okay?" he asked carefully.

I nodded.

"I'm going to climb off of you," he said and slowly let go of my wrists and sat beside me. "You're strong for someone so small."

I stifled a laugh and sat up, wiping my face dry. My nose in need of a blow and my head ached. "What happened?"

"You were dreaming. When I realized you were struggling to wake up, I had to do something."

"What did you do?"

"Well, I didn't think fucking someone vulnerable was very gentlemanly, so I just planted kisses everywhere."

"And held my hands," I added, noting the scratches

down his chest. "I'm sorry." I pointed at the marks. "Will they heal?"

"Soon, so don't worry your pretty little head." He cocked half a smile that melted my heart. "What were you dreaming?"

My cheeks heated at his rope work, then I shuddered, remembering the scaly man who morphed into his brother. I told Maddox about my dream, even about his room, and he listened intently.

When I finished telling him, a look of horror crossed his features.

"You're not safe around me," he said, climbing out of bed and pulled on his pants.

"What do you mean? Why is your brother trying to hurt you? And why did I dream about him?"

Maddox rubbed his temples, exhaling slowly. When he opened his eyes, he considered me with tenderness. Then a flurry of emotions crossed his face and I couldn't decipher them.

"If my brother has crossed over into your dreams," — he paused. A knot formed in my stomach, — "that means he knows about you and can find me. It won't be long until he arrives here," he said, pointing at the carpet.

"What happened between you two?" I asked carefully.

"I left home, and my family wasn't happy about it. They've wanted me to go back for years and I keep evading them. Until now." He pointed at his side.

I furrowed my brows.

When Maddox saw my confusion, he added, "My brother stabbed me with a knife used to collect souls. He wanted to trap me in the Underworld, but I escaped before that happened. But," — he rubbed his side, — "now I'm in constant pain and you're the only one who can keep it at bay."

His admission made me think about my ex. "Was Barry even at my house yesterday? Was I ever in danger?"

Maddox averted his eyes.

"Dammit Maddox, you lied, and you frightened me." My anger boiled to the surface, and I hated the way I felt. Too many had betrayed me, and I'd had enough. And now I'd slept with him, which made me feel used. Hurt. Like I was someone he could brag about to his demon friends.

"I'm sorry—"

"Get out." I yelled. When he didn't move, I slammed my fist into his chest and it felt like I hit a brick wall. I whimpered when my hand hurt. "Get out, Maddox. I'm sorry that happened to you but it's not my problem." It filled me with regret the moment the words left my mouth. I didn't mean them, but I hated being used. I valued myself as a woman. He couldn't think I was a toy he could use whenever he wanted.

Maddox didn't protest. He left without saying another word.

Chapter Twenty-Five

MADDOX

I walked the empty hallway of the club and my chest cavity felt just as hollow. I'd fucked up my chance with Kinsley and I had no-one to blame but myself. And the pain in my side kept reminding me just how badly I'd fucked up.

"Maddox!" Niki shouted, running towards me. "Man, am I glad to see you."

"Why?"

"A man was here asking about you and Kinsley."

"What man? What did he look like?"

"Kinda scrawny, missing a backbone."

Barry.

"What did he want?"

"He said a demon paid him another visit, that you'd know what it meant." Niki shrugged.

I flinched. That hollow cavity where my heart lived filled with anger. Levi was going to get to Kinsley through Barry, that he'd somehow discovered what she meant to me.

"You okay?" Niki asked, backing away from me. He raised his hands. "Christ, I don't know what that boy did, but I've never seen you this angry before——" Niki crouched in time.

I exploded into my true form; red skin, flaming yellow eyes, steel talons, long, whipping tail, large black wings, and my horns engulfed in demonflame.

"Maddox! No!" Niki screamed at the top of his lungs, cowering behind his arms under a table.

My wings expanded, demonflame burning atop. I roared in anger, burning everything within ten feet. I watched the tables and floor blaze, then just as quickly turned to ash.

My chest heaved as I struggled to calm down. I couldn't believe I was so stupid to let Kinsley out of my sight. Barry would lead Levi to her and then... I couldn't finish my thought. The outcome was too disastrous to contemplate.

"Maddox, my brother, what's got you so upset?" Mikhail asked as he entered the nightclub.

I crashed to my knees, morphing back into my human form.

"What did you do, Niki? Our friend is in pain." Mikhail squeezed my shoulder. "Tell me what my subordinate did to you?"

"It wasn't me," Niki said, coming out of his hiding spot. "But we have to help him."

I wheezed, my side continued aching like Thor himself had unleashed a thousand lightning bolts into my abdomen. Niki was right. I needed their help. It was impossible to take on Levi while I was in so much pain.

I stood, using a chair to keep myself upright.

"Tell us what's got you so rattled," Mikhail asked, his tone gentle.

I gave him a side glance. "Just don't go all soft on me, Mikhail." I chuckled, but that hurt too much. "Ah man, I need your help." My eyes flitted from Niki to Mikhail. "A friend is in danger and with this," — I pointed to my side, — "I don't think I can save her from my brother."

And if Barry was asking about Kinsley, it was a warning. I needed to go back to her house now.

Chapter Twenty-Six

KINSLEY

In order to get Maddox out of my mind, I kept busy with Mom. I gave Rosie the day off and I performed her duties.

Unfortunately, feeding Mom and ensuring I dressed her only took up so much time. Then I was back to thinking about Maddox and how he'd betrayed me. He was just another man who had used me for his own personal gain. He got what he wanted out of me by lying. I was nothing but a toy; something for him to use as he pleased.

I grumbled unintelligibly to myself, slamming the fridge door shut and sat at the counter. I sliced through my sandwich, picked up one half and enjoyed a satisfactory bite that left a sour taste in my mouth.

Unwanted emotions destroyed my moment of happiness; emotions I didn't want to feel. I didn't want to feel sadness, regret, or anger. I knew I had to feel something in order to move forward, but it was difficult. He used me.

Every time I wanted to hate Maddox, flashes of him came to mind and my heart fluttered with joy. There were visions of us as a couple, and I wanted to forgive him. Then the dream crashed down and replaced by the nightmare of him only wanting me to heal him. It was never about me as a woman with desires, but a healer.

He was never as interested in me as I was in him. I was sure this happened often; a woman completely and utterly into the man she dated couldn't see the signs showing his lack of interest or him wanting to end things. But he felt sorry for the woman and didn't end the relationship because he enjoyed the sex too much.

I shook my head in annoyance. In the short time I'd known Maddox, a part of me cared for him. It wasn't love, no, that was too soon. This part of me saw the good in people; the part of me that didn't need explanations or excuses and didn't judge; the part of me that put the other person's priorities before my own.

This was when expectations destroyed relationships, and I expected something from him—anything. But I knew it wasn't meant to be. He was not the right person.

That night he told me he was bad for me, he was right; I should've listened and stayed away. And I certainly shouldn't have slept with him. But...

I couldn't help myself; I couldn't stop myself when he touched me; when he lovingly caressed my body. I shuddered in delight. I should accept the experience for what it was; having sex with the devil's spawn and I enjoyed it. That's all it was. That's all it could ever be.

I raised my head and breathed deeply. Slowly, I was feeling better as I realized my self-worth. I had a lot to offer. I was tough and capable, and didn't wait for a man to do things for me.

I enjoyed another bite of my sandwich as the weight of my sadness and negativity lifted off my shoulders. I just had to keep thinking these positive thoughts. It would be hard but I could do it. I'd gotten out of my relationship with Barry, therefore it was possible to get over a sixty-second relationship with The Fixer.

I flinched when glass shattered somewhere inside the house and stood, knocking back the chair. I reached for the knife.

Another loud crash sounded upstairs and my skin prickled, my body iced over... Mother!

I darted up the stairs, but didn't get far. Barry's glowing red eyes stopped me in my tracks. When he grabbed my shoulders, I shoved my fist into his chest and winced. He didn't budge. His eyes glazed over yet seeing—this person wasn't Barry.

"Ah, here you are," someone said behind me.

I tried turning in the voice's direction but Barry's grip on my shoulders stopped me, burning my skin. I yanked out of his grasp, but he held on like a vise grip.

"Ow," I said, trying to escape again, but he was holding on too tightly.

Maddox's brother raised his hand, motioning for Barry to let go, and he did. I rubbed my arms where his touch had branded my skin, the smell of my burned flesh wafting in the air. I'd heal quickly, but the thought of Barry marking my skin made me sick to my stomach.

Maddox's brother stared fixedly at me, and an uneasiness spread within, forcing me to step away from both men.

"Now," Maddox's brother started. "I don't want to hurt you, but I will. Rather, come with me of your own volition or I will force you, and believe me you don't want me to touch you." He arched a dark eyebrow.

I raised my hands and approached him, not before glancing over my shoulder ensuring Barry didn't touch me again.

"Don't worry about him," Maddox's brother said. "The name is Levi." He proffered a hand, which I ignored. He stuffed both hands into his jean pockets and his sinister smile broadened. "Only trying to be friendly."

"What do you want with me?" I asked, my tone curt and filled with annoyance.

"Straight to the point. I like that in a woman," Levi said with a smirk. "Well, it's not really you I want, but my brother. It seems you two have become," — he paused for effect, waving his hands in the air, — "acquaintances and I need to ensure he comes home with me tonight."

The lines between my eyes deepened. "What's so special about tonight?"

He grinned and walked ahead without answering my question. His coat billowing behind him in slow motion, reminding me of a Nicolas Cage movie.

"Can I check in on my mother?" I asked, heading towards her room.

"Your mother is sleeping," Levi said, blocking my entrance. "If you don't come with me now, I'll ensure she never wakes up again."

I stared defiantly at him. He didn't budge. His eyes darkened. My vision blurred. His features morphed into the sinister creature he truly was, and I silently thanked the gods I couldn't see clearly.

I swallowed hard and blinked, turning away from him. My clothing clung to my body and the farther I stepped away from him, the cooler I became.

"I won't ask twice, Kinsley," Levi said gruffly.

Averting my eyes, I followed Levi down the stairs, with Barry close behind me. I shook my head, not believing I tried pushing my luck with the devil's spawn. If it wasn't Maddox, it was Levi.

I just wanted Mom and me to get away and enjoy a nice, relaxing holiday. We both needed a break from everything.

Levi opened the front door where a black van waited. The pocket door opened and scaly fingers reached out for me. I hesitated. Levi nudged me forward.

"He won't bite," Levi said with a wicked wink and climbed into the front seat. "Get in."

I shuddered, taking the proffered scaly hand and climbed inside the van with Barry too close to me. I pushed on his chest but hit a brick wall and he didn't budge.

"Not so close to me, Barry," I yelled and sat beside the scaly looking ogre who grunted.

Barry raised his hands in mock surrender and sat across from us.

The van jerked forward and Levi drove the vehicle down the driveway; he waved his hands, and the gates opened. Soon we were out on the open road.

Barry stretched his legs, his feet touching my shoes. I moved away from him, but he stretched his left foot farther until he touched my heel. The ogre slammed his fist into Barry's shin. A sharp snap sounded, followed by Barry bringing his leg to his chest, crying.

"What did you do that for?" Barry cried, swallowing hard in between sniffles. "What happened?" He asked, his eyes flitted between me, the ogre, and Levi. "Who… what's going on… Hey, I know you." Barry pointed a shaky finger at Levi. "No," — he shook his head, — "not again."

"You're an idiot." I folded my arms across my chest. "I honestly can't remember what I ever saw in you, but I'll make sure my baby knows what his father was really like."

"He?" Barry's eyes lit up like a decorated house at Christmas. "It's a boy," he said, hopefully.

"Doesn't mean you have a right, Barry. What you've done to me," I said, shaking my head. "You should be in jail. Or worse, maybe Levi must take you with him when he leaves." My words were cruel. I couldn't help it. I was mad. Angry. Furious. I was not a pushover and had lost patience.

The van smashed into something. Metal crunched. I flew into the back of the front seat. My head connected with the side of the van and the soft cushioned seat. Hands grabbed at me, pulling me away. My head throbbed from impact and all I saw was moving darkness.

Chapter Twenty-Seven

KINSLEY

Once outside the van, voices shouted, followed by punches. I struggled to see anything except sparkly stars. I felt the wet grass beneath me, a welcomed comfort, with the smell of mist thick in the air. Slowly, blinking vigorously, I started seeing shapes and colors once more.

Men wearing black clothing stood beside the van and another crashed vehicle; they had probably used it to aid Maddox by stopping Levi from getting away with me inside. I recognized the one from the club Maddox had taken me to, but I didn't know the others. They scared me but relieved they were assisting.

Maddox flew into Levi with a solid shoulder in his sternum and both devils flew into the van, crumpling it like tinfoil.

Beside me sat the scaly ogre with an unconscious Barry on his other side.

"You okay?" The ogre said, his tone deep but pleasant.

I froze. My eyes raked up the ogre's scaly, naked chest, then his face; which were all hard lines and deep ridges.

In the van I couldn't see him clearly, but out in the sunlight, I saw everything. He was ugly, yet strangely beautiful. His lips thick and his nose big and flat. His large brown eyes had seen centuries' worth of sad stories, while his skin a strange gray with scales that left a fine layer of ash everywhere. And on his head were large bumps instead of hair that looked sliced off. I'd never seen such a creature before, but curious enough to know more about him.

"Gorgon," he said, answering my question without uttering a word. "Levi rescued me from Medusa before she ruined me." He smiled sadly and rubbed the large bumps on his head. "Levi cuts off the snakes daily or they hurt me and kill anyone who approaches me. It's the only way to tame them." He scratched a red patch near his temple.

My chest squeezed as I listened to what he'd been through. No matter the type of creature, nobody deserved torture. There was enough hurt in this world, the Underworld, and the metaphysical world that any additional pain and suffering was overkill.

"I'm Mirreus." His lips curved upward, and the scales crunched and flaked off his face. I stared blankly as he scratched a flaky scale, only to have it float in the air like dust. He tipped his head towards the fight I'd forgotten about. "They've been fighting for longer than I can remember and neither wins."

Levi smashed through a wall of a ruined factory, escaping before the rest of the building collapsed onto him.

Maddox stood like the dark devil he was; chest heaving, sweat peppering his forehead, and his gaze raked up and down my body like he was searching for something.

"Are you hurt?" Maddox asked while scanning the area.

"I survived," I said, glancing at the gorgon.

Maddox tipped his head in appreciation and turned in time to block Levi's punch.

"Why are they fighting, anyway?"

"Maddox left the Underworld when their father needed him the most and since then they've struggled to take him back. Maddox has certain skills his father likes to use on lessor demons while Maddox hates using it."

"Oh, and what's that?" It piqued my curiosity and wanted to know more, especially since Maddox hadn't been forthcoming with information about his family or past.

"His touch causes permanent damage to demons and internal torture. It turns them into scaly creatures that their father hangs on his walls."

"It must hurt."

"You don't know what happened?" The gorgon arched both eyebrows and the scales on his forehead cracked and flaked.

"No."

"Maddox touched Levi earlier this week, and he had to go home to have their father fix him." He pointed at Levi, where I saw faint red marks on his neck. "He almost died."

I shook my head. My parents always supported my decision to become a nurse instead of following in my dad's footsteps and serve the council. I would rather heal than hurt, and I guessed Maddox was the same, although he traded his gift to help others for secrets or favors.

When gargling sounds caught my attention, Maddox kneeled on Levi's chest with his hands gripping Levi's neck. A dark gray cloud of dust surrounded Levi's body as scales spread across his skin.

Lightning crackled. Thunder boomed overhead. And the wind whipped debris in different directions, some of it hitting me, but with the large moveable gorgon to my side, he sheltered me from most of it.

"Thanks," I said when Mirreus turned towards me, blocking a large piece of tin roof from hitting me.

"You don't belong here," Mirreus whispered, shaking his head. "If you want to survive, say nothing."

"Wh—" I started, but swallowed my words when the large figure appeared out of the ominous clouds and floated to the ground. His sinister features left my mouth dry, and I was eager to hide.

Mirreus scooted closer to me, but the dark figure had already seen me; one side of his mouth lifted with a threatening twinkle in his eye.

"That's enough," the figure boomed. His voice deep and loud, making all the hairs on my body stand on end. "Maddox! Leave your brother alone."

Maddox did as instructed and stood up, stepping away from Levi.

Levi coughed, sitting up and scooting farther away from Maddox. He scowled at Maddox, who stood with his head held high.

"Why don't you come home, son," their father said, proffering a dark hand, talons outstretched. His raven hair blowing in the breeze while his large black and purple wings glistened in the sunlight. His blue eyes hinting at nothing pleasurable and everything painful.

Maddox shook his head. "Never, Seth. You know this."

Seth scowled upon hearing his son use his name. His outstretched wings shook as his anger receded. Seth rounded his broad shoulders and closed his penetrating eyes. It looked like he was counting to ten.

"You are my son, Maddox," Seth said with his eyes still closed. When he opened them, his demeanor had changed to something a little friendlier, although his words still cut like glass. "You need to act accordingly."

Maddox stared down at his father in response. His nostrils flaring and his clawed hands bunched into fists.

Seth's eyes flitted in my direction. Mirreus scooted closer to me; it overwhelmed me with joy how protective he was over me and he hardly knew me.

"What if we took your little slave with us? Would you follow me then?"

Maddox shook his head. "You can't. She needs to give birth to the boy I've already staked claim over. If she goes to the Underworld now, she'll lose the kid."

I froze. A solid knot formed in the pit of my stomach as bile rose into my mouth and I swallowed hard. Him claiming my child was the first I'd heard of and wanted to protest. I owed Maddox a favor. But this... this was cruel. This was not the favor I'd envisioned. I sincerely hoped he was joking; that this was some strategy Maddox was using to keep his father away.

Maddox didn't look my way.

Unshed tears threatened to spill down my cheeks. If Maddox was serious about taking my child, I couldn't protest. I'd given him my word. I should've stipulated what he could or couldn't take before agreeing. Not in a hundred years would I have thought he'd take my baby.

I flinched when something hard scraped my back. I glanced up at Mirreus's dark eyes, sensing comfort in them, biting my bottom lip to stop it from trembling.

Seth turned his frightful gaze towards me, and I cowered beside Mirreus. He shook his head. "You are truly my son." A sinister smile formed on his face. "Come Levi, let's go—"

"But, Father. You can't give up like that. We can still take him. Leave the bitch here—"

"No!" Seth yelled, swiping his hand in the air. Levi flew backwards, hitting the ruined building back first. He moaned as he tried to move off the rubble. "We will fetch him another day, Levi. If what he says is true about the kid, we will want him when he's born and we'll take them both. You know how I love a fresh soul, and male to boot." Seth's grin made me shiver.

Maddox just ruined my life and the life of my unborn son. Anger flooded my veins, and I wanted to rip out Maddox's eyes.

"I know you prefer young souls, Father," Maddox said 'Father' harshly. "Take my pain away," — he pointed to his side, — "and when the time comes, you'll get your young soul."

He used my son as leverage to take his pain away and not to rescue me. His discomfort. I should've expected his selfish nature would prevail.

Again, those feelings of regret, shame, and hate washed over me as I fought back tears while Mirreus continued rubbing my back.

I wanted to scream my frustration, to hit Maddox and to hurt Seth, but I was no match for either devil, and I could never hurt another; I wasn't the type of fae who could.

I choked on a sob and averted my eyes, focusing instead on the insects in the grass, the birds chirping, the stridulating crickets. His betrayal was too much to bear.

"I'll see you then, Father."

I glanced up when Maddox spoke and watched him approach.

Seth and Levi disappeared in a cloud of ash and the

wind died down. Mirreus evaporated along with them, leaving behind soot on the flattened ground where he was sitting.

"What the hell, Maddox?" I yelled. "What did you just do?"

"I had to, Kinsley. It was the only way they'd leave peacefully. If I didn't, Seth would come for you. I couldn't allow him to do that."

"What's going to happen?" I asked, rubbing my stomach.

The men wearing black headed in our direction.

"I have a plan. Trust me," he said with pleading eyes.

I wanted to trust him. I knew in my heart I could, but he'd only betray me again. I couldn't allow that to happen.

"How can you ask me to trust you when your behavior says otherwise?" I asked, my voice changing as I wiped tears away.

Maddox crouched before me. His expression softened, almost lovable, but I hated him. "I know I messed up, Kinsley, and I'm sorry. I shouldn't have treated you that way. I was wrong and shouldn't have let you go. Please give me a second chance and I will ensure your son's safety."

I didn't want to trust him again. I had to get far away from him and find someone to help me get out of this mess. But there was nobody else; The Fixer was in front of me.

My heart fluttered in my chest. Something akin to hope blossomed where a dark hole had formed, and I knew I shouldn't fill that hole with expectations.

"You hurt me—" I choked on the rest of the words as tears slid down my cheeks.

"Forgive me, Kinsley. I'm here now and won't leave your side again. Please," he pleaded, reaching for me, cupping one side of my face. I leaned into his warm palm and it felt safe, comforting, like home. "Can we start again? I have a plan."

I furrowed my brows and sat up. "Explain."

"I'll do better, I'll take you to her." He grinned, stood up, taking me with him.

"You ready?" The owner of the club said, I forgot his name, and I cared little to remember either.

"I'll take this one," said the other meaner, shorter, Russian. He motioned for two guards to take Barry. They picked up his unconscious body and carried him towards another black SUV type car—one I'd never seen before.

"Where are we going?" I asked Maddox as he lead me towards a shadowy corner, but he didn't answer.

Chapter Twenty-Eight

MADDOX

Kinsley and I stood near Mama's kitchen table. Mama mixed many ingredients into her pot along with hair, a few blood drops, and spit from Kinsley.

Mama said the incantation, her body started shaking and her eyes rolled into the back of her head. I glanced at Kinsley, who stood captivated by Mama's presence.

The two women bonded immediately upon meeting and Mama even pushed me away so she could whisper things about me I wouldn't say out loud. I left the ladies alone and made tea while they spoke in hushed tones near Mama's library.

Once they stopped speaking about me behind my back, I told Mama everything that had happened. She listened intently, nodding her head, and glanced at Kinsley with kindness in her dark brown eyes once I'd finished talking.

Mama had agreed to help Kinsley. She'd said we had a few options, but one was a certainty. When Kinsley heard this, she beamed.

I sighed with relief; hating that I'd caused trouble in Kinsley's life. I'd done many unspeakable things, but none this bad and never with an innocent soul.

If I thought about what I did, I realized this would be the only time I'd offer my life to set them free from my family's clutches. If it meant Kinsley and her unborn child remained unharmed, I would gladly exchange their lives for mine. I should've thought of that before…

I exhaled a frustrated breath; it was a selfish act to use Kinsley for a second time. Her anger towards me was justified. I deserved so much worse. It amazed me she trusted me enough to come to Mama's shop. But that's the type of woman she was; kind, generous, and put others first.

Something tugged at my chest, and I tried my best to ignore it. The burning sensation a heavy weight in my stomach. My hands itched. My mouth dry. All I wanted to do was hold Kinsley against my chest, whisper against her cheek how much I cared for her and that I'd do everything in my power to keep them safe. I should've done this a long time ago; before handing her over to my father on a silver platter.

"…Maddox," Mama yelled, slapping my shoulder simultaneously.

"Hmm," I said, my thoughts back in the present and my eyes flitted between the two women staring at me like my horns were showing. "What?"

The lines between Mama's eyes deepened. "Where were you just now? Never mind," — she waved her hands in the air, — "we're ready." Mama handed Kinsley the bottle but continued staring at me, shaking her head in disgust. I'd been around Mama long enough to know her thoughts by reading her facial expressions.

I glowered at Mama.

She narrowed her eyes at me.

I curled my lips, revealing sharp teeth.

Mama did the same.

Kinsley didn't notice our silent fight and excused herself to use the bathroom.

Mama pointed her thick finger at me, her whole body shaking. "I'm mad at you, boy. How dare you put that girl through so much. You just thought of yourself? I raised you better than that," — she shoved her finger into my chest, — "I sure as hell didn't teach you to be this selfish. You might as well go back," — she pointed to the ground, — "and join the rest of your awful family."

I exhaled, relaxing my shoulders. Mama was right. And I was taking it out on her too. "I know," I breathed. "That's why I'm here. I want to right everything."

"You better!" Mama shoved her finger into my chest. If she applied the right amount of force and moved her finger an inch to the right, she'd be able to dig into my ribs and remove my heart. I wish she would—but then Kinsley would become my father's toy.

"What's happening?" Kinsley asked, entering the kitchen. She stared from Mama to me and placed her hands on her hips.

"Nothing," I said before Mama spoke. "Let's go. I don't want my father changing his mind." What I didn't tell the ladies was my father could return with some of my brothers and they'd corner me and take Kinsley. I rubbed my side where Levi had stabbed me; the pain now completely gone thanks to the deal I'd made with Father, but the skin still tingled.

We left Mama's shop, and I drove us back to Kinsley's

home. As I pulled up the driveway, I parked beside the police squad car; both cops glanced up at the same time.

I told Kinsley to stay in the car and approached the police officers with caution; I didn't feel like digging out a bullet from my chest, and I certainly didn't want Kinsley to help me a second time.

"Good afternoon, officers," I said with a bright smile. I leaned against the open car window, peering inside. Both cops glanced nervously at me, opened mouthed, their half-eaten lunch still in their hands.

Using the powers that skated above the family line—and wouldn't send out a signal to my family that I was pulling power—I gazed knowingly at each cop. In my family, eye contact was as important as touch; the moment we looked at someone, we had their undivided attention.

"Go back to your station. Tell your captain that Miss Cavenaugh is safe, and the man harassing her will no longer be a threat. Now go," — I shooed them away, — "quickly."

Both officers nodded in unison. The driver took a large bite of his sandwich, threw the rest out of the window, and started the engine. He reversed out of the driveway and they disappeared down the road.

I dusted my hands, although there was nothing on them, and climbed into my Mustang. I started the engine and my car roared to life, put it into first gear and drove up the winding driveway, parking near the front door.

"Are you ready to do this?" I said, considering Kinsley. "Once we leave this place, you might not return." I tilted my head in the mansion's direction.

"When I have my mom, then I'm ready." She tried to smile, but the corners didn't quite reach her eyes.

She reached for the door handle, but I stopped her. "I'm sorry for putting you through all this—"

"It's okay." This time, her smile reached her eyes. "If I put myself in your situation, I might have done the same. You were desperate; injured. Anyone in the same predicament would do everything to get out. I get it," — she shrugged, — "come, I want to pack and go."

Chapter Twenty-Nine

MADDOX

I helped pack enough clothing for Kinsley and her mother, as well as all their valuables. The next thing on our agenda was trying to gain entrance into her father's safe.

Kinsley glanced over her shoulder at her mother, who stood with us. I doubted the old woman comprehended what went on around her, even though Kinsley was adamant she did. I would not argue with the woman; I'd been in her bad books enough times to know when to keep quiet.

"Mom," Kinsley started, then turned back towards the safe. "I think it's your birthday." She didn't wait for her mother to respond and punched in a date on the keypad I couldn't see.

When nothing happened, Kinsley mumbled to herself and punched in another number. "It's not your birthday or mine. Do you think it's dad's?" she said, sounding detached.

When nothing happened again, Kinsley approached her mother, placing her hands on her shoulders. "Mom?"

Her mother's eyes focused on Kinsley and something registered; she glanced at the award on her bedside table.

"Do you think it's the date he received the award?" Kinsley sounded annoyed.

"What did he get it for?" I asked.

"Some leader crap the council gave him. The only reason they did it is because of what's in that safe—" Kinsley pursed her lips and stared wide eyed at me.

I raised my hands. "I don't want them. Promise. This is for your family. I swear." This was one item I would not ask for. I'd done enough to mess her life up. And besides, she needed this more than I did.

"Do you promise?"

"Promise. Scout's honor," I said, crossing my heart with my finger.

Kinsley rolled her eyes. "I doubt you were ever a scout." She spun around and entered the date he won the award. The safe clicked open. Kinsley squealed and started packing the contents of the safe into a bag.

"Don't forget to pack your father's watch," the woman said beside me. I stepped farther away when the smell of her sour stench kicked up a notch.

"What is it?" Kinsley asked. She zipped the large bag closed and the safe behind her empty.

"Nothing," I blurted, thinking it best not to mention what my olfactory senses picked up. I didn't want to insult her mother, too. I still didn't know what caused it, and neither did Mama. Perhaps it was just me and my senses were changing; or I was changing. I shuddered, thinking of what that meant. Knowing my father, and not knowing who my mother was, anything was possible.

"Ready?" I asked

"Yes."

I followed the ladies down the stairs and froze on the last step when I sensed others on the other side of the front door. I wanted to stop Kinsley from opening the door, but I was too late. I silently cursed myself for not being aware of my surroundings.

"Detective Allen, Officer Mercer," Kinsley said, smiling sweetly. "What brings you here?" She glanced in my direction and I noticed an uneasiness in her expression.

"We'd like to find out about your ex and why you asked the cops stationed outside your home to leave?" Denis Allen said, stepping inside the home and forcing Kinsley to step backwards and almost into her mother. He didn't deserve to be called a detective, not after I'd seen what he did; helped his friend get away with murder.

When Denis glanced up and saw me, recognition flashed in his eyes, but then he frowned. I didn't think he could place where he'd seen me and I wasn't about to tell him.

I approached with an outstretched hand. Denis hesitated at first, but eventually shook my hand. "Hi, I'm a family friend," I said with my friendliest smile. I shook James Mercer's hand next; he was a pleasant fella. "I've heard you've done some great work helping Kinsley." I winked wickedly, and he flinched. It delighted me I could still make a grown man uncomfortable with a wink.

"Uh, well, yes," James said, his eyes flitting between Kinsley and me. "What Barry did was wrong."

"Yes, yes, what he did was super bad. But it's no longer necessary for cops to invade Kinsley's space." I interjected, puffed out my chest and stood in front of Kinsley, forcing the two cops to step outside again. I didn't want them seeing the boxes and mess inside.

James peered over my shoulder, arching both eyebrows,

and wanted to say something about the mess behind me when I grabbed his shoulder, forcing his eyes on me.

"There's nothing to see, James," I said in an ominous tone only he heard. Our surroundings slowed down as I gazed intensely into his eyes.

James nodded automatically. "Nothing to see," he repeated. When I let go of his shoulders, he blinked and licked dry lips. Our surroundings returned to normal.

Denis coughed with unease. "Shouldn't we maybe check inside?" he asked, trying to get back inside.

I narrowed my eyes. "Denis, Denis, Denis." I pushed past James and touched Denis's shoulder. He stiffened, most likely remembered where he'd seen me, and blinked back tears. The world slowed down again, with Denis and me in our little cocoon. "Do you want a one-way ticket to my father?" Although I would enjoy watching him squirm in one chamber reserved for the worst of the worst.

"Forget I said anything," Denis said normally.

I cocked my head to the side. Our surroundings remained frozen in time, yet Denis seemed blissfully unaffected.

"Tell me Denis, who got to you?" I glanced to my side, then over his shoulder.

His eyes darkened. I stepped backwards. I focused on Kinsley and using my mind; I whispered to her; she needed to drink the concoction Mama had made, close the door, and go. I felt her shift uncomfortably behind me. I didn't want to draw attention to her for fear the demon inside of Denis would attack.

There was movement behind me, then a door clicked shut. Denis and James turned dark eyes on me. I waited for them to pounce. They didn't. Billowing black smoke seeped out of their bodies and surrounded the two detectives like hot steam on a cold, rainy day. Smoke danced in the air above the cops and coalesced in the shape of a person behind them.

I fisted my hands. My skin rippled across my back; five centimeter horns grew out along my spine from my neck down to my tailbone. My black wings extended with a blue/purple shine depending on how the light struck it.

The billowing shape solidified and Levi stood like the pain in the ass devil he was. His red horns stuck out of his head in all its glory, his face contorted angrily, and his claws were out.

I flicked my black claws open and my steel nails lengthened, ready to remove body parts. My charcoal-gray horns extended. They were much larger than my brother's.

Levi seethed with anger; steam floated around his shoulders and neck.

My facial features morphed into my natural state while my frame grew. I rounded my shoulders and grunted; I felt relaxed in my natural form, no longer confined to a smaller body, and wanted to smile, but then I saw Levi and crushed my joy.

The two detectives fidgeted nervously. I gazed down at the tiny humans, puffed smoke out of my flaring nostrils. "I'd suggest you leave before you become road kill," I said in my deepest, ominous tone.

Both men nodded, then bumped into each other while sprinting away.

"Must you always save the humans?" Levi picked something out of his sharp teeth and flicked it off his nail. I shuddered to think who or what he ate.

"Only because I have a heart," I grumbled, stepping farther away from the closed front door.

Levi moved with me, ensuring I didn't get away.

"I knew you would double cross father. I told him my thoughts. He said I should see what you were up to. And low and behold," — he swept his right hand out like he was about to bow, — "what do I find? You and the woman trying to escape. Father will be livid when he hears this, Maddox. You constantly disappoint."

"Then go. If I'm such a disappointment, leave and let me be. You've wanted to be father's right-hand man since forever. Why bother with me?"

"You're the strongest, that's why. Yet since you've been here, you've hardly used your power. Are you afraid we'd pick up on your location?" he snickered. "You have the potential to become powerful enough that all supernatural's would bow down to you. Even father. Imagine?" He chuckled, but it sounded hollow. Jealousy seeped out of his pores; and I wondered if that's what caused the black ash.

I sucked in a deep breath, flared my nostrils and that same sour stench wafted in the air, but not as potent. Not like I smelled on the older humans. No, this was… I stepped forward, and the stink made me stop. It was Levi. His jealousy for me made him smell, leaking it everywhere, and even gave the human's foul body odor.

"What are you doing to the humans, Levi? Your smell; their smell, it's grossly the same."

A shocked expression crossed his features before morphing back just as quickly.

"I don't know what you're talking about."

"Don't be so coy, little brother. You reek of jealousy. But what I can't understand is why I didn't smell it on you when we first fought or why I smelled it on the older generations."

I barely finished my words when he lunged at me. But I was ready this time. When a shiny object caught my eye, I reached for Levi's wrist, twisting it. He cried out as he collided with me; his shoulder smacking into my side while I gripped his wrists, twisted, and drove the blade into his abdomen. Ending the fight before it started.

Levi crumpled to the ground solidly. Unmoving.

The wind whipped through the trees, whistling sounded as the wind blew through tiny holes and doorways. An angry wind formed, swirling around Levi and me.

I didn't trust Levi or the wind. I stepped backwards, unable to get out of the ring of disaster formed by the moving air.

Demonflame erupted through the ground like Mother Nature herself was ensuring we both burned.

"Ah crap," I said when the demonflame swallowed us both.

Chapter Thirty

KINSLEY

I stared at the closed front door and exhaled a shaky breath. I didn't understand what had just happened, but it relieved me we had separated from the cops.

When I opened the front door and almost walked into the detective, all the hairs on my arms stood on end, and he smelled like sour grapes.

While Officer Mercer had a strange way about him; his ruffled hair, creased shirt, and his left eye twitched. They seemed on edge and behaved strangely. I didn't want to wait and find out what they wanted.

Then, when Maddox whispered inside my head, I knew it was time to go.

I turned to Mother, who stood oblivious to what had just happened. "We must go," I whispered, gripping her shoulders tightly. "Hold on and don't let go." I dug inside my bag and pulled out the vial Mama had given me. I downed half the concoction and gave the rest to Mother. I grimaced at the acrid-grass-lemon taste.

My body tingled everywhere. Mother blurred around

the edges. I pulled the strap of the bag over my head, securing it in place, and grabbed Mom's shoulders once more.

Something registered in her eyes, and she gripped my elbows.

"You ready?"

Mom nodded, her smile not quite reaching her eyes, but she tried.

I felt as scared as she looked.

My skin glowed as a weight sunk into the pit of my stomach. Bile rose, and I swallowed hard, tasting the acrid-grass-lemon mixture again; making me shudder.

Heat blossomed behind my eyes; Mother blurred completely until she was only a thin plastic sheet and the house faded away.

Dark swirls surrounded us as we moved—dissolved—disappeared. I shut my eyes, expecting the apocalypse, and when we finally stopped moving, I opened one eye first, then the other.

The sun beat down on us. Tree branches danced with the light wind. Butterflies and dragonflies flew above us. The smell of wet grass and water assaulted my nose first. Then, when I focused on objects other than nature, Mother and I relaxed at the same time. We were home.

"Honey, we haven't visited in so long. How did you know to come here?" Mother said, letting go of my elbows. The smile stretching across her face made my heart swell with love. If I'd known she'd react this way, I would've brought her sooner.

"It was the voodoo priestess, Mom. Remember, I told you I was in trouble?" Mom stared vacantly once more, but I knew she heard. "She knew the devil or his demons have no direct access here." With so much going on, I didn't consider returning home. But I was ecstatic now that we were here.

Mother and I could enter fae world through our doorway at home, but it would provide Seth and Levi with a direct access if they followed my trail.

By drinking Mama's potion, I not only stopped them from following us, but diverted the trail that headed in another direction Mama had said would confuse them.

I snickered, imagining Seth's expression when they realized I wasn't where they expected me to be. It wasn't a permanent solution, but it gave us time to get the help needed.

I pulled on the bag handle, ensuring the contents were still there. I flinched when someone spoke behind us.

"Hey! How did you get here? Oh, Lady Beverley and Kinsley, please forgive me. I didn't recognize you," he said, approaching.

I turned around and smiled. Timothy worked with the council and my father; he couldn't cast a vote but he did a lot of the administration.

A glimpse at the building behind Timothy and my smile broadened. Mama had brought us right to the council's doorstep.

"Timothy," I said, closing the distance. "Just the fae I need. Can you help us?"

Chapter Thirty-One

MADDOX

Demonflame popped and sizzled as it sucked us into the Underworld. When we landed in my uncle's living room, the demonflame snapped and crackled as it disappeared, leaving smoke in its wake with nothing burned.

Levi grumbled on the floor as the knife slowly slid out of his body with a sickening pop. Once removed, blood pooled out of his mouth. He mumbled unintelligibly, but his eyes remained closed.

Uncle Victor entered the room with an air of authority; he ruled the Underworld and all the demons and devils within. He also ruled over his brothers and sisters and that included my father — Seth.

Although Seth was the oldest, their father had given each child tasks within the Underworld, but it was Victor who received the throne. Which Seth didn't appreciate and always tried to infiltrate and destroy anything Victor implemented.

Victor wore a pleasant expression, his dark suit fitting his gigantic form perfectly, and he reminded me of someone from a GQ magazine. He reached for the floating knife. Once it settled in his palm, it disappeared into sparkly ash until there was nothing but dust dancing in the air.

"Uncle." I nodded in greeting.

"Maddox, my favorite nephew; the thorn in my brother's side. What have you gotten yourself into now?" A hint of a smile tugged on his lips, then quickly slipped away.

"You know me, as much as I tried to leave this place, they just can't leave me alone."

Victor nodded curtly. "That is true. Unfortunately, that's what happens when you're born with unique powers others want to use."

I pursed my lips and bunched my fists.

"I don't want your powers," he blurted, raising his hands. "I do, however, want to piss off Seth and hopefully he'll leave you alone for good."

The tension in my shoulders eased, and I unclenched my jaw. "How?" I asked, the lines deepening between my eyes.

"A friend of mine can syphon another's power but instead of her trying to use it, I want her to place it into your brother," — he pointed at Levi who remained unconscious, — "and then he can be the object of your father's eye."

I nodded automatically as I thought this through. It might even work. "Would I still have that power?"

"Of course, my friend will only borrow some of it."

"Okay, I'm willing to try."

"Good, I'll be right back," Victor said, exiting the room.

I stood, staring at nothing for at least five minutes, before realizing I wanted to sit down. Casting an eye around the room, it was as I remembered; the vast living room boasted bright candles, sweet-scented air, and leather furniture that had been around for centuries.

The Fountain of Souls stood in one corner with the constant motion of water and the endless sounds of moans and screams took me back to my childhood when I used to tease the new souls. I'd tell them I could release them back to their bodies if they sang for me; I released none, but I heard many songs.

The Eternal Flame raged angrily in the fireplace; blue, yellow and red flames licking the sides of the furnace. I used to stick my hand in the fireplace when I was young and dumb. I knew better now.

Portraits hung on the walls. Ornaments collected over the years adorned on tables and against the walls; souvenirs taken when wars won and put on display for all to see how great the gods were; how great Victor and Seth were.

Sibling rivalry was a huge part of my childhood, not only among my aunts and uncles, but between my brothers and sisters. It got so bad that we almost lost our youngest brother because Levi was an asshole; I intervened and snapped Levi's arm, ensuring our smaller brother lived.

Not forgetting my powers. Powers so great my father threatened to kill everyone I loved if I didn't do what he wanted—the joke was on him because back then I loathed my siblings and I had no love interest.

And the powers in question hurt all demons; a scaly cancer-like disease that spread over their body until they were nothing left but a husk of their former selves. That within me, a darkness grew that even I was afraid of. A darkness my father had always wanted and envied. I rarely tapped into that part of me. It consumed the good parts of myself I didn't want to lose and I was afraid that if I used it again, I'd become what my father always wanted; a brainless killing machine.

My attacker backtracked, sucked in a breath and came at me again. He was relentless in his pursuit. But this was my job.

"If you come at me again, Paul, I'll hurt you," I said, my words threatening, and I meant it; this was what I did.

"I don't care," Paul barked. "Everybody runs Maddox. Your father is the tyrant we all despise, and I'm tired of following him. His old ways are going to see to his end. It's too late for him," he said, his tone softening "But it's not too late for you. Come with me," — he proffered an outstretched hand, — "and I will show you the world. You only know this life," — he raised his hands at the murky cave ceiling, — "you don't know the good I see in humans. Your father sends you out like a Pitbull, ready to attack and maul all without trial. It's wrong. Can't you see this."

I'd heard this story before and from many demons. I'd questioned my father once, and I barely left his chambers alive. Seth was an awful father; he was strict with his demons, but he was worse with his children.

"Don't listen to his pleas," Seth boomed behind me, making me flinch. "He's spreading false accusations. You know we can't have a divided house." His features darkened, and I knew that if I didn't do as he commanded, I'd get the demonflame lashing of my life. Anger and violence ruled our home. It's what we did, it's who we were. We punished those out of line and if we overstepped ourselves, we got it worse.

"You've had enough warnings, Paul," I breathed, closed my eyes and filled my veins with the darkness I pulled from somewhere deep within me. A power my father said I was the chosen one to receive, and that I should use it to protect the family, keep the others from tearing us down and hurting us. I did it to protect. I had to keep us safe.

My blackness seeped into my bones, filled my veins, and I felt invincible. I could destroy worlds with a sweep of my dark ability.

I didn't need to look in the mirror to know my eyes were black and my hair white; my potent power changed me in more ways than the obvious. A part of me slid back while the darkness took over.

I lunged for Paul before he blinked. My touch covered his skin in a thick, scaly skin that spread quickly. Paul only had time to suck in air when my power engulfed him, leaving his entire body heavy and stone-like. But that wasn't the worse part. Paul wasn't dead. My power trapped Paul within his body where he'd serve all eternity in a never ending torture chamber filled with days and nights of the same mind-numbing pain.

I finally let go of Paul when his eyes clouded over, his body stilled, left inside the husk of his former self.

My darkness receded, the color of my eyes returned, and my hair darkened once more. I lurched forward and vomited, narrowly missing my feet.

"That's it, get it all out," Seth said, keeping his distance.

I opened my eyes and the black slime slithered and seeped into the ground like the evil I'd conjured I couldn't contain after being used and it needed an outlet—out of my mouth.

Then, out of the corner of my eye, I watched Seth step farther back.

I wiped my mouth dry and stood straight. I cocked my head to the side; there was a nervousness about Seth I couldn't ignore and I wondered whether he was afraid of me, afraid of the darkness within me even though he wanted me to use it.

"What's wrong?"

"Nothing," he said, swallowing hard, then quickly schooled his features. "Before you leave, there's another demon against the family—"

"No!"

Seth's horns extended out of his head and his skin shimmered red. "Yes, you will."

Perhaps Paul was right. There were other ways to discipline demons and smiting them just because Seth said so was wrong. That Seth, my father, was wrong.

I coughed and more of the slime dribbled out of my mouth. I wiped it off with the back of my hand. I still felt nauseated. The evil I summoned each time I did that left me feeling worse until one day it would consume me completely, leaving me nothing but a husk. This outcome did not sit well with me and I knew I needed to change my destiny or I'd be nothing but my father's lap dog for all eternity.

"I can't do this anymore, father." I shook my head and stepped backwards.

"You can't leave your family, Maddox. We need you."

"No, you don't. The others can step in when you need help."

"But none are you."

"Not my problem. I can't do this anymore. It sickens me." I coughed again for added effect. "I'm done." I didn't wait for father's response and teleported to earth, to a place I'd always wanted to go—Sterling Meadow.

Blaire Thorne stared at me and frowned. "I think he's broken."

I hadn't seen this feisty human in ages and smiled. "It's good to see you, A-a-a-aunty Blaire."

"Ugh," she said, slapping my shoulder and brought me in for a hug. "I've missed you asshole."

"I didn't know you had powers," I said, squeezing her back. Blaire spoke a lot but said little about who she really was; she had enough secrets to fill this living room. I was the only one who suspected her and Victor's affair and never uttered their secret to anyone. She became my friend—as friendly as we could be—and Victor was the only family member on my side; I'd do anything for him.

"Well, it seems a lot is out in the open. So, shall we begin?" she said, clapping her hands and rubbing them together, reminding me of a crazy scientist.

Chapter Thirty-Two

MADDOX

I arched an eyebrow at the short beauty. Blaire stood in front of me with her hands on my naked chest and she glowed white. It was the strangest thing I'd ever seen. She glowed. White. Like a fucking angel. I knew her as this snarky, sarcastic woman who loved my uncle. And she could do this; it was strange.

"How many times have you done this?" I asked for the fourth time.

"Shh," she said, frowning. "I must concentrate. If you're going to interrupt the whole time, we might as well call Seth now."

"No, it's fine. Just be gentle. I bruise easily."

She snickered, opened one eye and I couldn't help but laugh. "I doubt that. But seriously now, let me concentrate."

"Fine," I said, exhaling, and relaxed my shoulders.

Blaire's hands warmed my skin. I rounded my shoulders as heat blossomed in my chest, followed by a sharp pull reminding me of a dentist extracting a tooth.

Blaire's power sliced through my body and I tried not to

flinch as it burned and she pushed more power into me. Sweat peppered my forehead. A headache throbbed between my eyes and panic struck a chord within my chest, making my heart beat erratically.

I opened my mouth to tell her to stop when air hissed around us. I convulsed. The air sucked out of my lungs. The darkness swooshed through my veins and moved through my body like molten lava.

My ominous power pulsed through me at lightning speed, and I was sure this was the end of me. My ears popped. Blaire removed her hands from my chest but continued glowing white; except her palms turned from their usual pink color to charcoal, then black.

Blaire paled as she stepped backwards with Victor guiding her towards Levi, who was still unconscious on the floor.

Slowly, Victor and Blaire crouched near Levi. A sheen covered Blaire's face and her hair stuck to her neck. Her green eyes were round as saucers and this was the first time I'd seen her afraid. She was as tough as they came. But not now.

Blaire swallowed hard, leaned on a knee and pressed her hands against Levi's chest.

Levi's eyes shot open, and he screamed as Blaire pushed my power into him.

His soul-piercing shriek made my stomach swirl, my vision blurred, and my ears rang.

Levi's ear-splitting cries continued as Blaire pushed every bit of power she'd taken from me and into him. Dark tears marked Levi's face. His skin ashen. And his body emaciated. He was dying.

"You're killing him," I cried, needing to get her away from him, but then I remembered all the shit he'd caused me and stopped myself from making a mistake. I had to trust Blaire and Victor. They knew what they were doing, and I waited.

Blaire finally removed her hands from Levi and sat back on her haunches, almost falling into Victor.

Levi laid there, unmoving, his body a dried up husk. I was about to give up when his skin plumped out like someone had breathed life into him. His skin no longer ghostly. Levi had survived the power transference.

Levi sat up like a vampire waking for the night and coughed; black ash sprayed out of his mouth and he shuddered. His eyes remained ink black with no white remaining; it was eerie and sinister.

"How you feeling?" I asked carefully, stepping backwards. If Levi was livid about the additional power, I didn't want to be in his firing line.

"I feel like a god!" Levi said, his tone deep and throaty. "I've never felt so powerful in my life." He stared at his palms, opening and closing his hands. He touched his chest, and I was sure I saw a blue spark.

Victor arched both eyebrows. Blaire stood behind Victor. And I smiled.

"Well, brother, now you can leave me the fuck alone."

"Yessss," he hissed. "This will please father."

"You'll leave me alone?" I asked.

"We don't need you anymore," Levi said. He always wanted to be Father's number one, and now he was. Father could always come after me again, but Levi wouldn't want to share the spotlight.

Speak of the devil and he'd arrive. The Eternal Flame roared angrily in the fireplace. Sparks flew, followed by a cloud of thick ashy-smoke. Seth appeared through the dense cloud with confusion stamped on his face.

"Brother, what have you done to my boys?" Seth said, shaking his head.

"Keep your panties on, *brother*. I've solved your problem."

Seth stared daggers at Victor.

Victor smiled, pushing Blaire behind him.

That was my cue to leave the family. I wanted to find Kinsley and tell her everything would be okay.

Chapter Thirty-Three

KINSLEY

We sat quietly in a room that was off the main council chambers. I enjoyed a bite of my scone, then wiped Mother's mouth clean. She seemed more alert and talkative, although she still wasn't quite the same.

Usually, when someone died, it was up to the family to notify their employer of their passing and if they were a supernatural; they had to inform the council. I'd been a little preoccupied with Barry stalking me, my mother falling silent, and Maddox and his crazy family after me that notifying anyone was the last thing on my to do list.

The council chamber doors slowly creaked open, and a hand waved me over.

"Mom," I said, waiting until her eyes met mine. "I'm just going in there quickly. This fae," — I pointed at our private security guard Timothy had appointed us, — "will take care of you."

"Okay, dear," Mother said, smiling nervously. She glimpsed her guard and sat back in her chair and stared out the window once more.

I exhaled audibly, stood up, and crossed the white marble floors towards the outstretched hand. I grabbed the wiggling fingers and Timothy gripped my hand.

"They're pissed at you," he mumbled for my ears only. "But, you've brought them a handsome gift and will most likely forgive you."

"Kinsley," Esmeralda said. Her green sleeve swept the table when she gestured I sit near her. I caught a twinkle in her emerald-green eyes. Her fiery red hair kept neatly off her face so I could see her sharp features. She was breathtakingly stunning, with no flaws that I could see. And when she smiled, her pointy ears lifted in joy too, brightening her face.

I sat beside her and surveyed the room. All the elders were here and stared at me like ravenous vultures. I'd only met them once before when I attended a ceremony with my dad; the night he received that stupid award. But other than knowing my dad worked on the council and most of their names, I only knew Esmeralda personally.

"We appreciate you bringing us this," Tagana said, lifting the bag with the important contents. Tagana was the council head and whenever I was in his presence, my fight-or-flight instincts kicked in.

I had removed our belongings from the bag before handing it over, and one other item not meant for anyone's eyes.

"As you can imagine," Tagana continued. "It disturbed us that your father had collected so much information about us over the years while he sat on the council." He shook his head disapprovingly. "Then, discovering many were on the receiving end of his malicious demands. Thank you for giving us these items without asking for anything in return. For your act of selflessness, we'd like to extend a hand to you and your mother should you need us. For anything."

What I'd learned from watching my father over the years was never directly ask for something but to suggest one thing that could lead to what you truly desired. It upset the elders that we didn't inform them of my father's passing in a timely manner, and we needed their help. There was no way they'd help us when we couldn't perform a simple task as required by the council. By offering them something so great, they had no choice but to offer the minimum in return.

"Naturally we'll destroy everything that's in here," — Tagana waved an elder over, one I'd never seen before. The elder stood up and approached Tagana, — "we have all gone over the contents and read what your father wrote so we know each other's secrets. By destroying this, we can't hold anything against each other. We have said vows we can't break. Now you need to be held in the same light.

"Unfortunately, only elders may say these vows. Therefore, we need to offer you your dad's seat on the council and have you say these vows, too. You don't have to take his seat every day. You may remain a nurse or whatever it is you do. The only time we'll need you is for formal gatherings."

His offer knocked the breath right out of me. I never wanted to follow in my father's footsteps and join the council, therefore I didn't know their rituals or who was new at the table. Also, I didn't care for politics, particularly fae politics; as underhanded and tricky as they were, I only wanted to help those in need.

But this... I didn't want to do. I could always tell Tagana that I never read my father's journals, but that was a lie and they'd never believe me, anyway.

I had to ponder their offer carefully because declining

could mean danger; if sitting on the council would afford Mother and me protection, then I had to accept.

Tagana placed the bag on the floor and the elder who'd approached crouched near it; sprinkling something on it.

Tagana stepped back.

The elder moved his hands over the bag. Flames erupted from the ground like the gates of hell had opened, burning the bag and its contents.

I leaned back in my chair; the heat beat against my body. I shielded my face for fear my skin was about to melt off. Then, just as quickly as it started, the flames died, and the room was again cool.

I sat up and stared at the pile of ash. A weight burned into my head and I glanced up. The elder's dark gaze left me uncomfortable. His lavender-colored eyes matched his lips and hair. His pointy ears larger than any fae I'd met, and his features sharp yet pretty for a male. He raised his hands and sucked in a deep breath, breathing in the ash until the floor was clean.

I wanted to grimace but feared judgement from the others, particularly the one who had cleaned the floor. I suspected he did more than just destroy items.

"What say you?" Tagana said, considering me. "About the offer."

"I accept," I said quickly, biting my lip to stop it from quivering.

"Good," Tagana said and clapped once, making me jump in my seat.

I felt Esmeralda's gaze on my left-hand side, but I dared not look away from Tagana. He reminded me of a snake you should never turn your back on.

"Right then, now that we've concluded important matters concerning your father, it's unnecessary for you to remain here today. We will send you a list of important meetings we'll need you to attend. We'll compensate you, of course, and you'll receive your father's powers." Tagana patted the same elder's shoulder. "Ambrose will source this for you."

I frowned. I didn't want my father's powers; they oozed evil, and it would always remind me of him.

"Don't you want them?" Tagana asked, his question dripping with disdain.

"My concern is it might alter my healing powers, therefore, if you agree, that I continue without my father's powers." I didn't know if this was true, but I hoped they'd agree.

"Very well," Tagana said, waving Ambrose away. "I agree with your concern. I've seen it happen before when two opposite powers combined. The strongest one remained and I suspect your healing powers would become muted under your father's power over death."

"Thank you." I bowed my head slightly and averted my eyes, sighing with relief. My father and I were complete opposites; I healed, he killed. I'd seen him brush his fingertips along someone's shoulders and they dropped dead—heart attack. He did this because they stepped in front of him when he wanted to walk ahead. It was only when he realized I was with, his twelve-year-old daughter, did he school his features and acted like nothing had just happened.

Before I could leave, they swore me into the council and I repeated the vows Tagana had mentioned. I expected something magical to happen to me, but nothing did, apart from a purple, dainty tattoo appearing around my wrist like vines, signifying my allegiance.

Tagana gave me a set of keys to a house they allowed

dignitaries to stay in when they visited. We could stay there for as long as we wanted and enjoy the security that came with it.

Esmeralda accompanied me to Mother, but before she left, she handed me a calendar with important dates scribbled on.

"I'm sorry for your loss, but I'm glad he's dead. He deserved it," Esmeralda said, but there was something in her bright emerald-colored eyes telling me she meant to say more. And when her eyes flitted to Mother, dread filled my veins. Esmeralda squeezed my arm reassuringly and hurried down the corridor, out of sight.

I didn't know what that was about, but suspected Esmeralda knew about Mother murdering Father. But something told me she wouldn't tell anyone. And it was the same feeling that told me my father had hurt her, too, and that she was glad he'd never return.

"Come, Mom. Let's go."

Chapter Thirty-Four

MADDOX

Fae world was another beast I was yet to conquer. They overflowed with riches, favors, and plenty of secrets, but that was for another time. I wasn't interested in them right now. I was only interested in Kinsley. I'd given her enough reason to hate me, but also hoped she would forgive me in time with the possibility of liking me again.

With Levi now my father's number one child, they could all leave me alone, which afforded me the time and freedom to do what I wanted peacefully. And what I wanted was beyond those gates.

Magical tall golden gates kept me out of fae world, along with big-ass fae guards standing watch. Both guards scowled when they saw me, aiming their weapons at my head. I raised both hands and stopped in front of them.

"I mean no harm—"

"You don't belong here, devil," Guard One said, cocking his weapon and keeping his finger on the trigger.

"As I was trying to say before you rudely interrupted me," I grumbled. "I mean no harm. Please, tell Kinsley

Cavenaugh that all is safe and well? That if she wishes, she may return home."

The guards faced each other and laughed; that throw-your-head-back-and-cackle laugh. I wanted to slap them.

"We'll do no such thing, devil," Guard Two said. "Now that she's a council member, all messages go through them. If they choose to notify her, they will."

I must've had a stupid expression because they laughed again.

"Get going before we use you for target practice." Guard One closed the distance and pushed his weapon against my forehead.

I'd fought my family for years and they messed with me when I finally met someone I wanted to open my heart to, open my mind, and open my soul. I wanted to offer it all to her.

My shoulders sagged as weight formed in the pit of my stomach and bile rose in my throat. I wanted Kinsley safe, but now that she's here, I wanted her with me. We could stay anywhere just as long as we were together.

It was presumptuous of me to think she'd stay anywhere near me. Perhaps it was best she stayed here; away from me.

I exhaled a shaky breath and pushed the guard's weapon down. "No need for violence. I'm leaving," I said, sounding deflated to myself. There was no need for theatrics and I wasn't in the mood to have my head blown off; fae weapons were the deadliest, and I'd die a very painful and gory death.

Although I deserved to have a worse fate than being shot.

If I thought about it, it relieved me that Kinsley was safe and her council had taken her and her mother in. And Kinsley would be much happier here without me. I'd only cause her more heartache and headaches. But I wouldn't be boring. I'd never cheat on her, or hurt her on purpose. I would only elicit certain sounds from her that would make her toes curl. Although once in a while she needed to nudge me in the right direction, but I'd always treat her with respect.

The devil in me was playful and mischievous. Luckily, I didn't have my father's mean streak. I suspected I was more like my mother; whom I'd never met and nobody had told me much about her either. Perhaps she was human and my father was too embarrassed to utter a word. She had most likely died during my childbirth and never had the chance to hold me, comfort me, bond with me. I was sure if she held me, I would remember her face and not just her voice.

As I walked away from the monstrous golden gates, I glanced over my shoulder one last time. The sadness I felt within was justified and welcomed; I deserved it, after all. I wanted to remember this feeling forever. That I ruined the chance of having something good and wonderful in my life. And the memories I had of us together burned in my brain for all eternity.

Chapter Thirty-Five

KINSLEY

I no longer needed to feed Mother or help her shower and dress; since we arrived in fae world, it did her a world of good; she was more alert, talkative, and her appetite had returned. She no longer slept all day and even walked in the garden.

A week had gone by and Maddox didn't return like he said he would. I surprised myself by my thoughts but if I were honest, I wanted him to let me know what had happened, that he was safe, that I was safe. I wanted to see him.

I hoped he had survived the wrath of his family and was safe. But there was nothing. I assumed everything was fine because no demons had tried to enter fae world, and if I wanted to know for definite, I'd go back.

Not wanting to become bored or give Tagana a reason to kick us out of the house, I wanted to understand the type of business the council discussed and attended their daily meetings. Tagana wasn't pleased, and I suspected he was considering kicking us out of the house anyway, but I didn't care. I was a council member, and they had to provide a good enough reason to expel me or an excuse not to allow me inside—which I doubted they'd do since I knew their secrets.

Esmeralda taught me council etiquette, along with who each member was and what they did. I could put faces to their secrets and understood why my father did what he did. It was wrong keeping damning information on each council member, but I now understood why he did it. They were vile creatures.

After spending hours with them, I didn't want to attend any more meetings and was content only attending important functions once a month.

I still didn't trust Ambrose, Tagana's so-called hitman. I enjoyed most fae company but there was something about him I didn't like and avoided Ambrose often, but sometimes it wasn't possible and I made it known how uncomfortable I was around him.

It was a late Friday afternoon, and I was glad to be done with the council meeting early. Mother walked around the garden and spoke with any fae who ventured nearby while I cooked dinner.

As I dished up, Mother entered the kitchen with a confused expression.

"What's wrong?"

"I was chatting with the guards, and they mentioned a demon had stopped by a few days ago and denied entrance—"

I dropped the pot and spoon; spaghetti Bolognese messed on the table, the pot broke a plate, and the spoon clanked on the floor.

"Why are we only hearing now?"

"I don't know. Maybe they forgot."

Or given instructions not to tell me. I thought of one person vindictive enough who would leave such an instruction. Rage filled my veins but also hope; the conflicting sensations left me dizzy.

"What did he want?" I swallowed hard and my heart raced in my chest.

"Something about it all being okay. Is this about what had happened? That guy you like? Uh, um, I can't remember the reason he couldn't stay."

"Yes, it's the reason we came here," I said, deep in thought. "That means it's safe for us to go back home."

"I don't want to go back," Mother said, her voice small and unsure. "This is my home."

"I want to go back, but I don't want to leave you by yourself."

"Tsk, don't be silly. I'll be fine." She patted my forearm. "You've spoiled dinner," she said, wearing a grin I couldn't help imitate. "I'll order food while you pack your things and we'll enjoy dinner before you leave."

Chapter Thirty-Six

MADDOX

A week had passed and I couldn't get Kinsley out of my mind; my hand fisting her brown hair with golden streaks while my other hand reached for her neck, my fingers curling around her slender column.

"You got it bad, man," Niki said, backing away from me.

I focused on the Russian and folded my arms across my broad chest, my clothing straining. All I did was lift weights this week, trying desperately to forget about her. It didn't help. Nothing helped. I wanted her. I needed her.

The thought of her willing submission clouded every second of my waking hour and haunted my dreams. Getting to know her body excited me to no end.

But that wasn't all.

I wanted her vulnerable before me while I seduced her mind. I wanted to write poems on her skin with my lips and have her crave for my touch.

I wanted that intimacy that reached beyond the physical and touched our souls as they entwined. To be thinking of her at a point in time and wonder whether she was thinking of me at the same moment.

I wanted all that and I wanted it with her and no-one else.

"Man, I've never seen you so depressed over a chick before," Niki said, scurrying to the bar. "You need more alcohol."

"No," I barked, pushing the drink farther away from me. One sip of the honey-whiskey and it left me nauseated. I didn't need to eat human food, but I wasn't drinking souls either; nothing sustained me. I ignored distress calls. Ignored anyone needing a favor. I even considered going back home and doing my father's awful work, but then everything I did would be in vain.

I combed my fingers through my hair and leaned against the chairback. "How's Mikhail? I haven't seen him around here?"

"Oh, you know, he's a very busy man now that he owns almost everything. Being the big boss doesn't come without its challenges, but he seems to cope." Niki placed a coffee in front of me, and I nodded my thanks. "Isn't there a way you can reach her without showing your devil-ass at those massive gates?"

"It's no use," I mumbled. "Anyway, this isn't a conversation to have with you. Stop asking questions," I grumbled, waving him away.

Niki stared for a heartbeat, not responding with a sarcastic comment. "Club opens soon. It's a big one tonight. Not sure you want to hang around, especially if you're in a mood."

I sipped my coffee slowly, setting the mug down, and climbed to my feet. He was right. I'd only cause trouble, and I didn't want bloodshed on my conscience as well. "I'll see you later." I sounded pitiful to myself, but didn't have the energy to clear Niki's memory.

Being a gentleman, Niki left me alone and tended to his staff.

I exited the club with my heart in my shoes, my mind on Kinsley, and my body moving automatically. I'd never felt numb before and wondered if drinking a bottle of chlorine would wake me up.

I shook the thought out of mind and pushed open the doors. The cool air smacked me in the face and I welcomed the sting.

I ignored the patrons begging to enter and strolled down the sidewalk. The dark evening sky was welcoming, but I hated the stars; reminding me of lovers as they glanced up together, enjoying each other while being blessed by the gods.

I didn't notice eyes boring into my back. I didn't feel the caress of the hand. And I didn't notice the tug of my heart-strings. But when she jumped in front of me; I noticed her then. My heart fluttered. My skin burned. And my smile stretched my face.

"Kinsley," I whispered for fear it was a dream. If I said her name louder, she'd disappear.

"Maddox," she said with a salacious smile, and my cock strained against my pants. I didn't want her to think all I had on my brain was sex and thought of something else instead of her naked body and her mouth on me.

"What are you doing here?"

"You didn't come to me."

"I was there, but couldn't get inside and I didn't think it wise to blast my way in there or I'm sure tweedledee and tweedledum would've used their guns on me."

Her smiled widened. "I only heard now, and I'm sorry. I

think they received instructions not to allow anyone in or to give me any messages. Anyway," — she shook her head, — "I don't want to talk about that. I want…" she bit her lip. "Are you seeing anyone?"

I shook my head and reached for her, bringing her in for an embrace. I bruised her lips with mine and my skin tingled with life which filtered throughout my body, and lastly to my heart. I felt every inch of her pressed against me, and I wanted to rip her clothing off.

"You want to go somewhere quiet?"

She beamed up at me and nodded quickly. "Yes." Her tone soft and filled with possibility.

I whisked her away to my apartment downstairs of the club, where it was quiet, and we could be alone.

We stood before each other, stripped of everything; our clothing and egos. We were simply two people; a man and a woman, attuned to what we wanted, and offered that part of ourselves to the other.

Kinsley agreed to feel the gentle strokes of my rope as I bound her, each knot perfect and tight. With her legs spread apart, I teased her slick folds until she came undone in my masterful hands.

Then I kissed her gently, nipping at her top lip, then her bottom lip. I devoured her mouth like it was the first and last time I'd ever kiss her again. And I wanted her to remember this kiss for all eternity.

Kinsley stood in blissful euphoria as I removed the rope. I carried her to my bed where, as much as I wanted to fuck her hard and fast, I made love to her. My strokes were slow and with purpose. I wanted her to feel all of me as I felt her; not only my body, but my soul.

The look in her eyes told me everything I'd always

wanted, always needed. That she truly was the one for me and I hers. There was nobody else I wanted.

And in that moment we reached a balance; in mind, body and soul; aligned in harmony and peace.

The darkness that swirled within me, bled away as Kinsley's light engulfed me.

Kinsley embraced her heavenly strength as a woman and reveled in her femininity.

Me—the devil—a demon, but also a man; a gentleman secure enough in my masculinity and confidence. And knowing the difference between arrogance and using my dominance to have her do things at her own free will.

When our two halves met—heaven and hell—the purest form of beauty washed over us. Our souls met in perfect alignment. And when we added our love, we created something every writer and musician had written and sung about for years.

Our orgasms struck at the same time as waves of pleasure caressed over us. I held onto Kinsley; her damp skin against mine, and I didn't want to let go.

When the sensations dissipated, I pulled her into the curve of my body where we laid like that for a while. We spoke about our feelings. Spoke about our future. And spoke about a family.

And as we revealed our raw emotions, the love I carried for Kinsley only grew, and I knew she was my one true love.

Chapter Thirty-Seven

KINSLEY

My throat was hoarse. My body ached like nobody's business, but love engulfed me. I held my little bundle in my arms as he slept peacefully.

Maddox had fallen asleep in the visitor's chair, which was funny considering he rarely slept. I guessed watching me give birth took everything out of him. Luckily, he didn't have the man-flu, or he'd be in the bed beside me.

"Hey," Mother said, entering the private room. She placed the vase of flowers on my bedside table. "How was it?" She kissed my forehead and pulled the blanket down to look at him.

"It was okay," I said, brushing dirty hair out of my face; I needed a bath, but right now I didn't want to move for fear of waking him. "It was a struggle, then everything happened quickly. He was out, crying, and now he's in my arms." I smiled tenderly.

"What's his name?"

"Nolan."

"Unusual name, but I like it. What's wrong with him?"

She tilted her head in Maddox's direction, trying not to laugh. "He looks exhausted."

"He rushed putting the baby room together, and without using his magic. He said he wanted to do everything himself, and he even painted the room."

Maddox had gone above and beyond his duties and not just a boyfriend. These last eight months, he consistently did things for me without having to ask. He was everything I'd always wanted in a husband and father to my children. And he couldn't wait to make one of his own when I was ready, but he would love this child as if it was his own. He also said he wanted ten kids, and that's when I had to apply the brakes. Four kids were plenty. But we'd cross that bridge when we got there.

"How's home?" I asked. Mother still lived in fae world and I doubted she'd ever move away again.

"Everything is good, I've joined a knitting class."

"I knew the fae were weak," Maddox said, sitting up and wiping his face with both hands. "But knitting is just ridiculous."

"Huh, the devil's spawn awakes from his slumber and you didn't give birth. I wonder what that says about you," Mother grinned.

"My father called. He needs help in hell's kitchen."

"Ha, you're so funny." Mother poked Maddox in his shoulder. "Well, dear, I'm not staying. Bridge class starts soon and you know I hate being late."

"I appreciate you coming to visit," I said. It took effort for Mother to come all the way here to see her grandson, and I knew she wouldn't stay; twenty minutes in the human world was all she could handle. I suspected the memories of my father in this world were too much for her and she felt safer in fae world. "We'll visit you soon."

Mother kissed my cheek.

Maddox stood up and hugged her. "Don't break a nail on those cards, Beverley. I'd hate to see you beside your daughter in hospital."

Mother rolled her eyes. "I don't know what you see in this one." She poked his shoulder again but spoke to me. "Are you sure you want to keep him? Is he house trained or does he need a diaper too?" She grinned. "I can always drop him off at a shelter."

I laughed. "Bye mom."

"Bye," she said, waving over her shoulder and slipping her arm through her guard's arm and they disappeared down the hallway.

"At least this guard has stuck around longer than a week. Do the fae know she abuses them?" Maddox sat on the bed beside me. "How's he doing?"

"Fine," I said, handing the human bundle to Maddox, who took the boy with care.

Barry was no longer in the picture, and Maddox had confirmed he'd never return. Apparently, the Russians had taken care of everything for us, and I was grateful for their help. This boy would know Maddox as his father and only when he was old enough to understand would we tell him about the sperm donor—but, with all things, anything could change.

Seth and Levi hadn't bothered us again. The day after we moved in together we received a parcel from Seth wishing us well. Maddox almost collapsed. It seemed Seth didn't want my son's soul after all but has requested Maddox visit the Underworld once a year with Nolan. Apparently Seth wanted his grandson in his life. I didn't want Nolan accompanying Maddox, but we'll see; it all depended on whether Seth continued to behave.

"Are the doctors happy for you to leave?" Maddox stood up and paced, rocking the baby.

"Yeah, I've healed already." I swept the bedding off and climbed out of bed. It wasn't necessary for me to give birth in hospital, but the head nurse insisted on ensuring my safe delivery.

I dressed and stood near Maddox, who stared at me the entire time while he tended to Nolan.

"Let's go," I said, leaning my head against his arm. "I'm ready to start the rest of my life with you and our kid. And maybe practice making the next one."

"Seriously?" he asked, eyebrows raised.

"You-bet-ya." I kissed his cheek and sashayed out of the private room. "Well, come on, devil, I'm not repeating myself."

Kai: Chapter One

KAI

I entered the hallway and into the cavernous room. I assessed whether any of the doors had been breached or if any artifacts Léon stored in his renovated warehouse had been stolen or damaged.

Everything was as it should be and stepped into the kitchen I shared with three other shifters. I switched on the kettle and added a tea bag into my favorite mug. A smell caught my attention, and followed the stench to the basin; inside sat dirty dishes and leftover food with flies buzzing around. When I opened the dishwasher, it was full, too.

While the kettle boiled, I burst through Jude's door and the were-tiger jackknifed out of bed, his fists out readying to fight.

Jude narrowed his eyes, realizing there was no threat, giving me the middle finger. "Asshole," Jude said, raising his hands above his head to shield his eyes from the blinding lights. "I was sleeping."

"It's your turn to empty the dishwasher."

Jude groaned and fell back into bed. "You're worse than my freakin' mother. Give me ten more minutes."

"Now, Jude, the kitchen stinks. Do you want cockroaches again or worse, the stench of rotten food hovering throughout the warehouse?"

"Christ! All right, all right, I'm up," Jude moaned, kicking off the covers, and climbed out of bed. He pushed against my chest as he stomped past. He headed in the kitchen's direction, scratching his ass as he made a show of how upset he was that I disturbed his sleep.

Jude reluctantly opened the dishwasher tray and unpacked the dishes into their rightful spots while I finished making tea.

"Morning." Lee strode in, flicked my ear and darted to the other side of the kitchen, narrowly missing my backhand.

"One day I'm going to get you where it hurts."

"I can't wait. Maybe then you'll get that old man stick out your ass," Lee said, drinking water from the open faucet, then closed it.

"Someone needs to keep you in line or this place would be in chaos and Léon would bleed you dry."

Lee grunted.

"Morning." Flynn entered and roared. He removed a mug from the cupboard and started making coffee. "You should rather drink this, Kai," — he tapped the coffee pot. "It gives you great hair." He combed his fingers through his jet-black hair.

Lee laughed. "Man, I still find it strange your mane goes sun-soaked yellow when you change."

"Yet, it stays gloriously dark around the edges." Flynn wiggled his eyebrows. "The darker the mane the more powerful the lion," he roared again.

"We get it," Jude mumbled. "It's not necessary to rip out the measuring tapes every morning, we all know you're the *bigger* animal."

"We're quicker though." Lee elbowed me.

I nodded. "That may be true, Flynn, but I prefer tea," I said, placing my cup on the table. "You two still okay for tonight?"

"Yes," Flynn and Jude said simultaneously.

"I'd do anything for you to get laid and to get off my back about the dishwasher," Jude mumbled into the dishwasher and closed it. "I on the other hand am always happy." He arched an eyebrow, no doubt reminding us he always had a lady keeping him company. "'Cause at night the monster ladies love to come out and play."

"Yeah, and they steal from the Master," I said dryly.

Jude harrumphed. "It happened once, Kai. Are you ever going to drop it?"

"Maybe when you start doing your chores without us having to ask you."

"Why can't we get someone to clean around here."

No-one answered Jude because we had this conversation with him numerous times before. Léon had already advised against anyone or a cleaning company to clean the warehouse because of the nature of the items he stored here.

Cleaning up after ourselves was part of our job. And besides, no-one would want to clean up after a bunch of animals, anyway; I grinned at the thought, leaning into the chairback.

I listened to the other men's banter and quietly sipped my tea. Jude was into any woman who would have him, while Flynn was a picky. Lee and I had been so busy lately we hadn't had time to find women. Hopefully tonight we'd break our dry spell.

As the others joked around a part of me wished I had found my mate. I wasn't an alpha male who led the pack, but a beta male who ranked high within the were-leopard leap, along with my best friend Lee. Beta males did what was necessary to keep the pack strong and followed through on alpha orders. And it was beta males who usually only found their mates later in life or worse yet, never at all. And since I was not a natural born were-leopard, my chances were slim.

Every time I heard about beta shifters finding their mate, it left a sour taste in my mouth. Although I didn't have many one-night stands, I was getting tired of them. In today's world of quickies and hook-up culture, I still hoped my *one* was out there waiting for me.

I wanted someone to bond with, to share my life with and to cherish forever. The thought of waking up next to the same girl every single morning made my heart swell.

I wanted to know everything there was to know about that one woman. I wanted to commit every line on her body to memory. To know what made her scream my name as we made love. Sharing our thoughts for the future, and maybe even kids.

I wanted all of that and more. Unfortunately, I would have none of that.

I learned not to expect anything on my night out with Lee, and tonight would be no different. Lee might find a girl interested enough in him and bed her, or he'd just do it at the club. While I usually stood by the bar and drank.

Going out was more for Lee's benefit than for myself. And even though Lee knew this, it didn't stop him from dragging me along.

A hollow uneasiness settled within my chest but I made peace with it. This was my life now. I would forever be alone, a dedicated worker to the Master Vampire of Sterling Meadow, and committed to Sebastian who led the leopards.

Kai: Chapter Two

KAI

I stepped out of the shower as Lee waltzed in the communal bathroom with only his towel slung over his shoulder.

"I hope you're ready for all the ladies we're about to meet?" Lee said with a mischievous smirk. "And you got enough rest."

"You're bad for my reputation," I said, keeping up with the bravado. When I reached the door, I added. "It's not like we haven't been out before."

"I know we've been out. It's just we've only been to Léon's clubs and I'm tired of fangers. Have you decided where we're going first?"

"I thought you had a place in mind."

"No," he said, furrowing his brows.

"Okay, let me ask Jude then, he knows them all."

Once dressed, I found Jude eating in one of the private rooms. He sat in a chair made of gold with engravings etched into it.

I whistled. "Léon is going to murder you when he sees

these recordings." My eyes flitted to the cameras in each corner.

Jude always ate in this room; he said he felt like a king. He rested his feet on the golden coffee table while he ate chow mein out of the box.

"You know he never checks. Besides, you do such a stellar job here that nothing goes wrong. And he trusts you." He shoveled a mouthful of noodles. "Unless you plan on telling him?" he added as he chewed with bits of sauce spilling down his chin.

"Not yet, but if you continue using it as a dining room, I will. Anyway, that's not why I'm looking for you. Which club would you say is the best one? We've kinda lost touch with what's out there and one that doesn't belong to Léon—"

"There are a few, but my favorite is owned by the Russians. But don't go there though. They don't like our *kind*." He arched an eyebrow.

"I knew the Russians were in town, but I didn't know they already owned a nightclub."

"They were quick, but oh my gods, it's the best one. Again," — he pointed his chopsticks at me, — "do not go. Those guys are crazy and will kill you. They only allow humans in."

"How do you get in?"

"I enter with my human friends. It's the only way. They have a bear bouncer to sniff out the riff-raff. Just don't let him catch your leopard stink. Maybe blend in with some women and their perfume. He's one of a handful of shifters allowed on the property, and he is one vicious animal. I saw him rip apart a were-rat in the alley. It was nasty stuff, man." Jude shuddered and shoved the chopsticks into the box. "Thanks, you just killed my appetite."

"Give me the addresses for the other clubs and include that one. We might drive by."

"Sure, but don't do it, man. If you don't know how to blend in, it's not worth it." He stared at my clothing. "You might get in." One side of his mouth curled upward.

Kai: Chapter Three

KAI

I entered *Spiders* nightclub first, with Lee trailing behind me. There was no dress code or entrance fee. Which usually meant one thing—the riff-raff frequented here.

The place smelled of cheap cigars, alcohol and vomit. In a corner stood two men wearing leather; their ears had large flesh tunnels in their earlobes adorned with black earrings. They had snouts instead of noses as they had partially shifted into their hog beast.

A woman danced on stage, or rather slithered. Her tail rattled as she danced. When she reached the center of the stage, she gripped the pole with four arms and pulled herself up, an arm let go of the pole, removing her top. The hard rattles at the end of her tail shook and vibrated hypnotically. Her skin as smooth as porcelain and her raven hair cascaded passed her shoulders. Her breasts natural and firm.

Lee gawked at the snake-lady. I nudged him and he wiped his mouth dry.

"Oh my gods, she's beautiful."

"And deadly horned. Look at her head."

Lee raked his eyes up her body, her breasts, then widening them when he saw the two horns on either side of her head.

"She's deceptively poisonous. I would advise against meeting that one."

Lee shuddered as he forced himself to look away. "I need a stiff drink." He corrected the bulge in his pants and turned toward the bar.

I chuckled knowing Lee was easy to please when it came to women—they all did it for him. I on the other hand had a type and reptiles weren't it. I knocked twice on the wooden counter to get the barmen's attention.

"What's your poison?" the bartender said when he reached us.

"Two double shots of Tequila." I left money on the bar while the bartender poured our drinks.

I elbowed Lee, pushing his shot closer to him. "To all the pussy cats you gonna meet," I said, winking wickedly and downed my drink.

Lee downed his drink, scrunched his face at the awful taste and slammed his glass on the counter, alerting the barmen for a refill.

"I hate those things, but it gives me such a buzz. It's just unfortunate we have to drink a shit-ton before it does anything," he said, grinning.

The bartender refilled our glasses, Lee paid for this round.

We downed the shots, slammed our glasses on the counter simultaneously and turned around, scanning the dance floor. Men sat along the walls, with only a handful of women in-between. A couple stood near them, one in the corner, and then there was the magnificent snake-lady on stage.

"I must be honest. This place doesn't have enough women," I said with disappointment.

"Yeah, let's go to the next place."

The next nightclub had a queue all the way around the block. Lee grumbled when he saw it went right around the second block as well.

"There's no way we're getting in there tonight. Right, what's the next one."

The next establishment was the same as the first one; except it had more drunk men than women. We exited with a half an empty bottle of Tequila.

"Now what?" Lee asked, finishing the liquid and throwing it in the trashcan. "I don't discriminate, but I prefer the delicate touch of a woman. That place," — he thumbed behind him, — "was just too much testosterone for me."

I glanced at the list in my hand. There was only one place left. "We could try this one." I pointed at the word.

"*Stingray*," Lee sighed. "I've heard about it. They might not welcome us."

"We can go to one of Léon's clubs or back home—"

"No way. We're always going to his clubs. I love them, they have desirable women but they're mostly vampires. And I don't want to go back to the warehouse. It's still early. Let's check out *Stingray*," — he shrugged, — "maybe it's not so full."

I drove slowly past *Stingray* nightclub; blue, yellow, and green lights alternated as they struck the glass with their colorful strobes. I felt the music vibrations all the way to our car. Smoke emitted out the entrance as the bouncer spoke to a group of ladies.

I found the closest parking spot and killed the engine. Glancing over my shoulder at the warehouse, I had a sense of uneasiness spreading through my body. The tall dark bouncer flexed his impressive muscles as he pushed a man to the curb, pointed at something in the distance as he yelled at him never to return. The man crawled to his car and drove away.

"Maybe we shouldn't." I squeezed the door handle but kept it closed.

"It will be fine. We're cats, we run faster." Lee climbed out and slammed the door.

I hated when Lee did that; he assumed just because we're shifters, we could run away from anything. We could do a lot more than humans, but we weren't immortal; we'd die someday. It was just a matter of how much trouble we'd be in when that day arrived.

I ran my fingers through my short brown hair and exhaled sharply. I scratched the stubble on my chin and doubted I was in the best condition to catch any woman's attention.

We'd been working non-stop the last few years with hardly any time to play. With Sebastian and Greg becoming the alpha leaders of the leap, I knew we would be needed there and at the warehouse. Flynn and Jude were excellent shifters, and we got on, but... they were sloppy. And we desperately needed a break.

Finally, I gave into temptation and climbed out, locking the car.

It was risky entering a human only nightclub. As much as I wanted an evening away from leap and vampire business, being recognized as a shifter inside this club could result in our untimely death. This was a Russian nightclub after all, and they didn't take lawbreaking lightly. Lee and I had been best friend since the start and helped each other when trouble found us, and tonight wouldn't be different.

The mountain of a bouncer glowered over the line of patrons waiting to enter *Stingray*. We stood behind a group of rowdy men when two women came into the line behind us, smiling sweetly.

Lee elbowed me, wiggling his eyebrows. He turned around and started speaking to them.

The line moved up. The bouncer came in my line of sight. The four men in front of me laughed and joked. Two of them whistled at ladies who walked past to join the line behind the other girls. They blurted obscenities at the ladies, who blushed in response and avoided eye contact with the group of men.

The bouncer pointed at me. I glanced over my shoulder. When I turned back to face the bouncer, he approached.

I grabbed Lee's forearm. Lee stopped talking. The bouncer reached for us, but instead of taking hold of me, the bouncer grabbed the man in front.

"If you can't behave here, there's no way you'll behave in here." The bouncer pointed at a sign on the wall that read, *'While you wait, please do so respectfully'*.

"Hey man, everybody chill. We're cool," the man said as he placed a calm hand on the bouncer's shoulder. "We're all friends here."

"Don't touch me," the bouncer growled, pulling the man out of the line and shoved him away. "Get away before I pummel your faces into the concrete."

The man who had spoken raised his hands and nodded.

"Yeah, sure. We're going. No harm, no foul." He pulled on his friend's shirt. "Let's bounce."

The men crossed the road and climbed into a Maserati Levante. They were far too young to afford something like that. They barely had facial hair.

The bouncer returned to the front and allowed a group of women to enter.

Lee continued flirting with the two women behind us, but instead of joining their conversation, I stared at the men sitting in the Maserati. They didn't leave. They glowered at the club as they spoke. No doubt conspiring to do something.

When we finally reached the front, the bouncer gave us the stink eye. Then his eyes flitted to the two women hanging onto us, he allowed us access.

I was grateful Lee could be charming when he wanted to. With the girls help, we were able to access the venue. It wasn't as if we were trying for territory by pissing against the wall to lay claim to the building. We came for a good time.

As I stepped through the door, the heat smacked me in the face and the music was loud. Sweat beaded on my forehead and dripped down my back.

I followed Lee and the two women to the bar and ordered another round of Tequila shots.

The redhead, Kimberly something, clung to me while laughing at Lee's silly jokes.

I should be enjoying myself, but I wasn't. There was something indescribable about tonight I couldn't put a finger on. It wasn't the redhead pawing me like she'd never held a man before, but something else. I could almost taste it in the change of atmosphere.

I glanced around the club and that hollow feeling inside

intensified. Perhaps it was the part missing a mate, or I was having an off night. But the more I thought about it, the hollower I felt. And stranger thoughts swirled inside my head.

In all the years I'd been a shifter, I always felt as though a part of myself was missing. Whether it was parts of my soul, or the human part I'd lost, but the feeling sharpened tonight. There was something here that stirred within my chest, to the point that it ached.

I glanced at Lee who carried on like he always did—full of jokes and smiles—nothing disturbed him.

"Let's dance," the redhead said, pulling on my hand.

I groaned inwardly, not feeling like dancing, but didn't want to be rude either. She was pleasant looking with big brown eyes and long red hair. I followed her onto the dance floor anyway, with Lee and her friend beside them.

The music drowned out my thoughts as we danced. My body moved, but I didn't feel the music like I should. It felt superficial and forced. And I felt removed from my body not understanding why.

Lee gyrated against the woman beside him.

When I heard the redhead's name was Tiffany, I didn't care. I wasn't interested in her or her friend and would soon forget their names.

I danced, trying to feel the rhythm of the music in my soul, but it wasn't there. Casting an eye around the room of moving fevered bodies. The sweaty humans laughed, drank and danced. A woman had fallen to the ground without spilling her drink. Her partner helped her back onto her feet and they careened toward an empty chair. The smell of sweat, alcohol and arousal filled the large building.

One thing I realized surveying the humans, they were slow, docile creatures; weak and stubborn. When someone bumped into me, slurring an apology, I didn't push back. My shoulder sagged as I thought about leaving the dance area to blend with the shadows.

I reached for Lee to tell him I was sitting down when my eyes locked on her legs; toned and curvy. My heart skipped a beat as my eyes swept over her from heels to head; she wore a knee-high skirt that hugged her hips and ass, causing my body to twitch. She wore a low-cut white blouse with a black lace bra peeking through the see-through material.

I swallowed hard, but my throat remained dry.

She glanced from one side of the nightclub to the other, searching. Her neat raven hair shoulder length, framing her cerulean-colored eyes and delicate features.

Lee grabbed my shoulder, bringing me out of a trance.

"Hey, man, what are you gawking at?" Lee asked, glancing over his shoulder. "Oh my gods, no wonder you're drooling. I'd fuck her right on the dance floor."

"Hey!" I slammed my fist into his chest. I felt protective over her and didn't understand why.

"Ow man, it's just a saying. Christ. She's definitely a ten. Go speak to her while I keep these two company. Or, I can go to her and you take these two?" Lee said with a sly smile.

Not needing encouragement, I pushed Lee aside, turned, and slowly headed in her direction.

Grab your copy...
www.vinci-books.com/kai

About the Author

A Multi-genre author writing twisted endings...

N Gray is a USA Today Bestselling Author who lives in Cape Town, South Africa, with her daughter and adopted cat named Miss Beans.

During the day, she's an analyst and provider profiler for a medical insurance company. At night, she types on her curved keyboard, creating fictional characters some may love and others you want to kill yourself.

She writes in four genres: urban fantasy, thriller, horror, and paranormal romance.

She now writes under Natalie Michaels for her new thrillers and SD Syns for her new horrors.

Acknowledgments

With special thanks to Rabea and Karin.

And thank you to Tammy at Book Nook Nuts.

Thank you to my readers, old and new, for taking a chance on my books.

You are the reason I write the stories I do. As long as you keep reading, I'll keep writing.

I'm truly humbled by your support and encouragement.

I write in as many genres as I love reading in. There are so many stories swarming inside my head that I could never just choose one.

Horror is my guilty pleasure. I love writing short stories filled with dark humour and the occult, with a twist ending.

Urban fantasy and paranormal romance are where I love to spend my time, and I have so many books planned that I don't have enough time *(but I'll get there)*.

And lastly, my thrillers. Who doesn't love sitting on the edge of their seat while reading about what goes on inside the antagonist's mind? Well, I love writing about them.